Photo. John Flower

HAROLD CHILD

Essays and Reflections

BY

HAROLD CHILD

EDITED
WITH A MEMOIR BY
S. C. ROBERTS

CAMBRIDGE
At the University Press
1948

Printed in Great Britain at the University Press, Cambridge
(Brooke Crutchley, University Printer)
and published by the Cambridge University Press
(Cambridge, and Bentley House, London)
Agents for U.S.A., Canada, and India: Macmillan

CONTENTS

Contents

The *Critical Essays* and *Christmas Reflections* are reprinted, by permission, from *The Times Literary Supplement*; and *Ephemera*, similarly, from *The Times*.

MEMOIR

I think my first meeting with Harold Child was in 1912, when he came up to Cambridge, as dramatic critic of *The Times*, for the performance of the *Oedipus Rex*. He was an old friend of my predecessor at the University Press (A. R. Waller) and Waller suggested that I might like to go to the Greek play with him.

Thus began a friendship of more than thirty years. Child was a keen and intelligent lover of music and followed the score of the choruses with quiet enthusiasm. Hypocritically, I pretended to share his intelligence. I remember, too, that in the early days of the 1914 war Child came up to Cambridge to collect some notes on the university in war-time. I helped him to meet some informative people, but it was not until after the first war that my intimacy with him developed. Gradually I saw more of him both in London and in Cambridge and gradually I learnt more about his life and work.

Born in 1869, Harold Hannyngton Child was the son of Thomas Hannyngton Irving Child, Rector of Stratton, Gloucestershire. He was in college at Winchester and won a scholarship to Brasenose. At Oxford (where one of his best friends was George Bancroft, son of Squire and Marie Bancroft) he took a second in Greats and was subsequently articled to a firm of solicitors in Thornbury. At Thornbury he was in his home country: 'there were horses to ride, and lawn tennis, and picnics, and skating at Tolworth, and the two hundred acres of rough shooting at Earthcott that one of my uncles had lent me, and dancing, and private theatricals'. But when he was sent to the office of his firm's London agents, he quickly sought a way of escape from the prison-house. George Bancroft told him that he was 'much the best' of a group of amateur actors at Hampstead and John Hare gave him the part of 'a Guest' (at 30*s*. a week) in a new play by Sydney Grundy—*The Slaves of the Ring*. It was the first play criticized by Mr Bernard Shaw in *The Saturday Review*, but as Child's part was 'a jewel, two words long', it escaped the critic's notice. The play was a failure and Child was advised 'to go into the provinces and get Experience'. The story of that Experience, of touring as the Light Juvenile Gentleman with Harry Paulton in *Niobe*, of playing the part of Lawyer Sly Fox in pantomime and of many other adventures is told in *A Poor Player* (1939), a little book which gives a fascinating sketch of the theatrical milieu of the nineties.

Child's stage career ended after two years and he had already begun to write. At the house of James Welch, with whom he had acted in *Niobe* and *In a Locket*, he met many members of *The Yellow Book* group and among them Richard Le Gallienne, who introduced him to the editorial office of *The Star*. For that paper he wrote a series of short stories and his first book was a novel, *Phil of the Heath* (1899). It was a romantic tale of the Reform Bill period and I suspect that Child regarded it as one of his growing pains. But it was all part of his literary apprenticeship and Child, as one of his obituarists remarked, was by nature a man of letters. He became assistant editor of *The Academy* and later of *The Burlington Magazine* and he was dramatic critic of *The Observer* from 1912 to 1920. But the main course of his literary career was in fact determined by his association with his old friend Bruce Richmond in the inception and development of *The Times Literary Supplement* in 1902. Of the *Supplement* he became a mainstay and gradually his contributions to *The Times* increased. For many years he acted as lieutenant to A. B. Walkley in dramatic criticism and he confessed in later years that he could not help imitating him. But Child was no imitative writer. Whether he wrote as critic, or special correspondent, or light leader-writer, his work bore the mark of his individual quality, of his fine sensitivity alike to the humour and to the beauty of life. Like Dr Johnson and Mr Bernard Shaw and other good judges, he recognized no fundamental distinction between good journalism and good literature, and one of his friends has recorded that if he caught himself in the act of introducing a cliché into an article, he tore up what he had written and began afresh. The quality of his *Literary Supplement* criticism led to his being invited to contribute a number of chapters to the *Cambridge History of English Literature* and the chapters covered a wide range of subjects from the Elizabethan Theatre to Fielding and Crabbe and Jane Austen. In the stage, and especially the Shakespearean stage, he retained an abiding interest. Walkley had told him that his short experience as an actor enabled him to give the acting a proper place in the pattern of his dramatic criticism. Similarly, in his approach to Shakespeare Child remembered always the actor's and the producer's points of view and his stage-histories were a distinctive feature of each volume of the *New Shakespeare* up to the time of his death.

But, apart from the theatre, Child was keenly sensitive to the imaginative element in poetry, or painting, or music, or travel. The books that he wrote, though slim in bulk compared with the great mass of his work as a journalist, are a fair index to his literary sympathies: there are guide-books to Shakespeare's country and the Channel Islands; there are translations of *Aucassin and Nicolete*, of Bremond's *Sir Thomas More* and of Dimier's *French Painting in the XVI Century*; there is the libretto of Vaughan Williams' *Hugh the Drover* and a small book of love poems, *The Yellow Rock*. Most of these were written before *The Times* absorbed the greater part of his literary energy. Only once, I think, did he reprint a series of newspaper articles in book form. It was a series of essays which appeared in the Woman's Supplement of *The Times* and it was published as a book with the title *Love and Unlove* in 1921. I do not remember that Child ever talked to me about this little book and I can guess why. The essays are lay sermons and he did not love the role of preacher. Quietly and frankly, these essays face the problems of human life and human relationships:

Put briefly and roughly, what I have come to believe is that the main source of strength, activity and happiness is human love. These terms, too, need some defining. By happiness...I do not mean comfort nor contentment. Traherne's little poem says the last word on the difference. Contentment is 'a sleepy thing'; it is a state of negation. Those who wish to be contented can achieve it pretty easily, like the aesthetes, the sentimentalists, or the merely selfish and lazy, by shutting out all the people and things and thoughts which they find disagreeable. Happiness is not a negative measure of shutting out, but a positive measure of taking in more and more.

And again, in words that remain painfully apposite:

Let us suppose the worst. Let us suppose that our present civilization is doomed—doomed to go to pieces in blood and fire and to give place to an era of barbarism. It will be mighty unpleasant to be blown up, or shot, or starved, or robbed or all together. But men have endured these things without losing their faith and their hope —even their happiness—because on a different plane they have achieved their end, and in regions outside material things have gone as far as circumstances would allow them to the realization of themselves.

Such was the starting-point of his approach to literature as well as to life. 'I will confess', he wrote, 'to a passion for contemplating Utopias', but he contemplated them with his feet on the ground. Though a large part of his working life was spent in criticism, it was impossible to conceive of him making an enemy. Of course he had his own opinion of second-rate writing and of books which need never have been written. Once, when I quoted the remark of some trans-atlantic comedian: 'Boy, even if that was good, I shouldn't like it', he seized upon it with delight as precisely applicable to some of the books that came his way. I think he positively disliked the writings of Hugh Walpole and he thought Galsworthy's novels overrated. But, for the most part, he preferred to look for what was good either in a book or a play and to make his criticism a 'positive measure of taking in more and more' of the author's message.

Afflicted in later life with recurrent asthma, Child was debarred from many of the physical pleasures that he had enjoyed in earlier years. But there was nothing in him either of the invalid or of the ascetic. He had a proper sense of the pleasures of the table and loved to share a bottle of good wine with a friend at the Garrick. As a companion he was at once restful and stimulating—I suppose because he was a superb listener; but against the prohibitions of Puritanism he could become almost violent. I remember that when he came to a small dinner-party arranged to celebrate the publication of *The Name & Nature of Poetry*, he was delighted when Housman remarked: 'The only form of Christianity I profess is anti-Protestantism.'

In his last years his health grew worse. He retired from whole-time journalism, but not from writing. The English winter tried him more and more severely, but he spent most of his time in London until his flat in Buckingham Gate was bombed. In 1942 he had a serious illness, but his spirit remained buoyant. In December of that year he wrote to me from the Westminster Hospital:

I only see people whom I must see or whom there is no chance of my seeing when I am at home again. And as laughing is as much discouraged as talking, you are one of the very last people I should think of asking them to let in.

You and I and a bottle of Burgundy—it is an entrancing, a rosy prospect! But when, Lucius, when? I am Perfect Patient Number One. Doctors and Sisters and such come and gloat over my chart, which seems to have, like some modern poetry, an inner beauty appreciable only by the initiates....When I get home (they swear it shall be before Christmas) I shall be no good for a time. In January Nell and I are to go to Brighton. When I get back from there, I shall be pushing buses over and drinking like George Augustus Sala. Then you must look out for yourself!

He recovered—not to the extent of pushing buses over, but sufficiently to carry on some of his literary work. On one of my last visits to him I found him sitting up in bed, very wheezy, but quite cheerfully reviewing a book of Shakespearean criticism. In August 1945 he wrote rather wistfully of the doctor's chances of finding 'an elixir of youth with retrospective force' and in November of that year he died.

The essays contained in the pages that follow cannot pretend to represent fully the range and the content of Child's scholarship. They take no account either of his biographical work or of his dramatic criticism. What they do attempt is to give just a hint of the clean and scholarly style which he preserved even in his lightest pieces; of the gentle, humourous spirit which pervaded them; and of the faith in spiritual values which underlay them. For to Harold Child belonged the *anima naturaliter Christiana*.

S. C. R.

CRITICAL ESSAYS

THE TRIUMPH OF BEN JONSON

(1936)

The test of Housman's razor would find very little pure poetry in the big and beautiful book of Jonson's poems newly edited and printed by Mr Bernard Newdigate.[1] Such, at least, is the impression left by a study of the whole of the contents: the reprint of the *Epigrammes* and *The Forrest* from the folio of 1616, and of the *Underwoods* and the translation of the *Ars Poetica* from the folio of 1640; Mr Newdigate's own gathering of what he aptly entitles 'Drift-Wood' from many books and manuscripts, an 'Anthology' of poems rather strictly selected from the plays and masques, and a 'Farrago' of scraps by or about the poet. Very seldom has the reader's skin bristled, his throat closed, his eyes watered or the pit of his stomach been pierced. Indeed, this masterful man, Benjamin Jonson, has so held him in thrall that he feels it almost disloyal to take any heed of what may be accidental, not deliberately intended and worked for. It is no merit in the blackbird that his song makes the flesh of the hearer 'go goosey', whereas the song of the thrush does not; and if Jonson's poetry can make the reader 'go goosey', he may easily feel like one who in the theatre has laughed in the wrong place He has a vision of the terrible old poet roaring at him that such haphazard sensibility is worse than any wolves' black jaws and dull asses' hoofs.

Housman's razor, moreover, is not so sure and constant a test as Occam's. It must be used unawares or not at all; and the effect of taking thought about it, of asking oneself whether its action—whatever physical form that may take—was felt or not, is uncertainty like that of one who, listening with all ears to a distant nightingale, ends by not knowing whether he

---

[1] *The Poems of Ben Jonson.* Edited by Bernard H. Newdigate. Oxford: Blackwell.

hears it still or not. In Jonson's poetry there are a few, a very few, famous beauties, short poems or passages which are familiar in song, or may be found in most anthologies. When the reader met them in his journey through the book, was the thrill—if any thrill there was—one of immediate magic or only one of recognition of an old friend? The natural result of thinking about it is to be diffident about the magic, *Drink to me only with thine eyes*—beautifully wrought, indeed, and a noble piece of rather arrogant courtiership; but empty of all spontaneous feeling, particularly that of love—all the more clearly so to the eyes, skins or stomachs of those who can tell how Jonson has changed the tender entreaty of his original, *Philostratus*, into the statement of an accomplished fact. *Queen and Huntress, chaste and fair*—that lovely thing has so wound itself into the affections that it arouses now not so much the thrill of rapture as the deep peace of love; yet surely in that last verse:

> Lay thy bow of pearle apart,
>   And thy cristall-shining quiver;
> Give unto the flying hart
>   Space to breathe, how short soever:
>   Thou that mak'st a day of night,
>   Goddesse, excellently bright.

the magic is not all that of the thing suggested, the eternal magic of moonlight, but is partly at least the magic of the very words, of the pure poetry. 'See the Chariot at hand here of Love'—here he is simple, sensuous and passionate indeed; and no lover that knows it but has wanted to crow aloud, out of his own triumph, the last verse; but the simplicity is won at the cost of depth, and it leaves none of the mystery and the reverence which are the pure stuff of love poetry. Housman himself found his razor respond to the first lines of the elegy on Lady Jane Pawlet, Marchioness of Winton:

> What gentle Ghost, besprent with *April* deaw,
>   Hayles me, so solemnly, to yonder Yewgh?
> And beckning wooes me, from the fatall tree
>   To pluck a Garland, for her selfe, or mee?

4

But when such reactions are being tested, it is easy to wonder whether Housman did not pitch upon those lines partly because Pope imitated them very badly, and Housman was just then as eager to trounce Pope as to exalt Jonson. 'Still to be neat, still to be drest'—it is delicate and deft to admiration; but there is no magic in it. 'It is not growing like a tree'—the heart leaps to it, because it is so much nearer pure poetry than all the rest of the Ode in which it is but a 'Turne'; but Herford and Simpson, as wise in judgement as they are firm in fact, have it right. The lily quatrain has true lyrical charm; but 'the opening couplet states a truism with the emphasis only proper to an illuminating truth'; and the last couplet is 'more proper for discourse than for song'. Besides the well-known pieces and passages there are less familiar things in the big book which give the thrill of surprise.

> The faiery beame upon you,
> The starres to glister on you;
> A Moone of light,
> In the Noone of night,
> Till the Fire-Drake hath o're-gone you.
> The Wheele of fortune guide you,
> The Boy with the Bow beside you,
> Runne aye in the way,
> Till the Bird of day,
> And the luckyer lot betide you.

That is all that Mr Newdigate prints of a song in *The Masque of the Gypsies*, which, though not published till 1640, was performed in 1621. *The Night-Piece, to Julia* was not printed till 1648; but Herrick was in London till 1628 or 1629. It would not be fair to take it for granted that not he, but Jonson, invented that tune; but the odds are very heavy in favour of Jonson, from whom Herrick certainly borrowed as well as learned.

> Slow, slow, fresh fount, keepe time with my salt teares;
> Yet slower, yet, o faintly gentle springs:
> List to the heavy part the musique beares,
> 'Woe weepes out her division when she sings.

5

Droupe hearbs, and flowres;
Fall griefe in showres;
  'Our beauties are not ours:
    O, I could still
  (Like melting snow upon some craggie hill)
    drop, drop, drop, drop,
Since natures pride is, now, a wither'd daffodill.'

With so much in the book to drive us forward into the age which Jonson took the lead in creating, it is more than pleasant to fall back, with that, into the old ways; and the other song out of *Cynthia's Revels*. *O, that joy so soon should waste!* has at least a touch of that lost Elizabethan lyricism mingled with its almost Restoration pride of the flesh. This taking of thought, this self-examination in the physical reactions leads, perhaps, only to one complete disappointment— the song which Gifford thought the finest in the English language:

Oh doe not wanton with those eyes,
  Lest I be sick with seeing;
Nor cast them downe, but let them rise,
  Lest shame destroy their being:

O, be not angry with those fires,
  For then their threats will kill me;
Nor looke too kinde on my desires,
  For then my hopes will spill me:

O, doe not steepe them in thy Teares,
  For so will sorrow slay me;
Nor spread them as distract with feares,
  Mine owne enough betray me.

Skin, eyes, throat and stomach remain utterly insensitive. The examinee deserves full marks for his exercise; but not one of his 'sons', not a single Cavalier lyrist of them all in the new Jonsonian era could have produced anything so inhumanly frigid. On the other hand, there is one, and perhaps only one, complete triumph; and so unexpected as to suggest that there must indeed by something in this test by Housman's wholly unintellectual and irrational razor. It is impossible to read the Epitaph on Salathiel Pavey, 'a child of Q. El. Chappel', without feeling all the symptoms. The poem is 'conceited'; it is mythological; it is frankly false in the means that it uses to express its sentiment. But the queerness is not explained away by saying that, in spite of the false expression, the feeling is genuine. It is not the feeling—not the conception of the great poet grieving for the death of a loved, clever and gracious little boy—which produces the symptoms. It is something in the very words themselves. The poem moves, by conceipt after conceipt, to a plainly conventional conclusion —and the effect of the whole is like the effect of music.

So much about the Housman razor—merely to see how Jonson's poems—poems in the sense of this book's title-page— stand a test for which they were never intended. The effect is to show Jonson not a smaller but a greater poet than the other tests show him without it, because, even more than with his friend Drayton, sincere labour for other poetical ends has won here and there a gleam of celestial light. It must not be forgotten that in this matter of poetic magic the ancients have a ground of complaint—against Shakespeare, of course, but also against the successors who have so often of late years complained of them for unfair competition. The romantics, and the inheritors of the romantics, have spoiled us. Coleridge, Shelley, Wordsworth, Blake, Tennyson, Meredith—these are all magicians by design. They sought, expected and waited for the breadth of the power that, for Abt Vogler, framed out of three sounds not a fourth sound but a star. Their conscious contrivance of beauty of sound is no true measure; or Pope would be beyond question the greatest poet of all. The secret must lie rather in their attitude to life. They had what George Saintsbury called the upward countenance. They looked (it is a hackneyed phrase, but true) with wonder; they looked with admiration and reverence. That attitude is found in poets by no means romantic or happy-hearted. It is the condition of all the tenderness and wistfulness that underlie the pain and sorrow in Hardy. It is the condition even of Housman's own fastidious savouring of life above and below the mean. The

7

attitude is rather passive than active. Such men desire rather to receive life—to 'experience' it—than to mould it to their own pattern. Of them Jonson was not one. His thoughts of womanhood and of love are alone enough to prove it. All the evidence offered by these poems of his is epitomized in his remark to Drummond: that Donne's *Anniversary* was profane and full of blasphemies (Jonson's own blasphemy, in his Royal addresses, was of a different kind); he told Mr Donne, if it had been written of the Virgin Mary it had been something. Jonson saw all life without mystery or cause for reverence; full of clear detail, a definite matter that could be shaped by any brain and will that were strong enough. When he consumed a whole night in lying looking to his great toe, what he saw in that rapt state of imagination was Tartars, Romans and Carthaginians fighting. We remember that another poet 'saw Eternity the other night'. The nearest that Jonson comes to that shows the wide difference. It is a little complimentary poem in James Warre's *The Touch-stone of Truth*, included by Mr Newdigate in his 'Drift-Wood':

> Truth is the triall of it selfe,
>   And needs no other touch.
> And purer then the purest Gold
>   Refine it neere so much.
> It is the life and light of love,
>   The Sunne that ever shineth,
> And spirit of that speciall Grace,
>   That Faith and Love defineth.
>
> It is the warrant of the Word,
>   That yeeld's a sent so sweet,
> As gives a power to Faith, to tread
>   All false-hood under feete.
> It is the Sword that doth divide
>   The Marrow from the Bone.
> And in effect of Heavenly love
>   Doth shew the Holy one.

After that, Jonson, as so often in his poems, catches sight of the particular object, the detail of fact, and lurches down on to it, just as in his *Epithalamia* or his *Elegies* he will lurch down to details of the marriage service or of a pedigree. But at least he has climbed to no small height, and has been using something more than his strength of judgement. That little poem is wider-winged even than the well-known and almost purely beautiful poem *The Mind* in the series in which the old poet mourned the death of Lady Venetia Digby, the woman who, if not alone, above all others roused in him feelings of veneration with some suggestion of spirituality. 'Great Jonson did by strength of judgement please'; but the poet who wrote the opening of *The Hind and the Panther* could not have failed to recognize in great Jonson something more than strength of judgement. And seeing how he can surprise and delight with such moments of revelation, the reader becomes more and more reluctant to decide that there is anything in this book which Jonson could not have written. *Underneath this sable hearse* is very probably not his but William Browne's; but the internal evidence is far from strong. This doubt becomes more important when the question is of the four Elegies, *'Tis true, I'm broke!*, *To make the Doubt cleare that no Woman's true*, *That Love's a bitter sweet*, and *Since you must goe*, of which the second appears also among Donne's *Elegies* as No. xv, *The Expostulation*. The problem cannot be discussed here; but Mr Newdigate is certainly not to be condemned as foolhardy in arguing, against such authority as Herford's, that all four Elegies may be not Donne's but Jonson's.

In the end, however, Jonson would be judged not by the exceptions in his work, and still less by any test involving the uncertainties of personal fancy, mood, or predilection. He has definite things to say, and his object is to say them as compactly and pointedly as possible. His enlargement of the epigram is a commonplace of literary history; and, in a sense, in nearly all his poems he is trying to write epigrammatically. Suggestions of infinite lights and glooms, though they happen, are not his care. There is a world about him of fact, full of particular people; and in that world good things and bad things, good people and bad people are clearly different and

9

can be clearly expressed. The art of poetry becomes to a great extent the art of compression.

> Jephson, thou man of men, to whose lov'd name
>   All gentrie, yet, owe part of their best flame!
> So did thy vertue 'enforme, thy wit sustaine
>   That age, when thou stood'st up the master-braine:
> Thou wert the first, mad'st merit know her strength,
>   And those that lack'd it, to suspect at length,
> 'Twas not entayl'd on title. That some word
>   Might be found out as good, and not *my Lord*.
> That *Nature* no such difference had imprest
>   In men, but every bravest was the best;
> That bloud not mindes, but mindes did bloud adorne;
>   And to live great, was better, then great borne,
> These were thy knowing arts: which who doth now
>   Vertuously practise must at least allow
> Them in, if not, from thee; or must commit
>   A desperate solœcisme in truth and wit.

He has packed his suit-case; and he can shut it without kneeling on it. But some of the clothes—and very good clothes they are—have been a little clumsily folded and remain creased. We turn the page and meet with this:

> If I would wish, for truth, and not for show,
>   The aged *Saturne's* age, and rites to know;
> If I would strive to bring backe times, and trie
>   The world's pure gold, and wise simplicitie;
> If I would vertue set, as shee was yong,
>   And heare her speake with one, & her first tongue;
> If holiest friend-ship, naked to the touch,
>   I would restore, and keepe it ever such;
> I need no other arts, but studie thee:
>   Who prov'st, all these were, and againe may bee.

When Dryden said that Jonson, compared with Fletcher, wanted ease, he was not thinking of his poems, or here in that one 'epigram' would have been his sufficient refutation.

The world has heard enough of Jonson as an influence. A great influence he was; and part of the pleasure of reading his poetry is to see where others have drunk of his cup: but he accomplished poetry as well as influenced it. The world has heard enough of Jonson's crabbedness. He is very often crabbed. But the effect of Mr Newdigate's book is to drive the crabbedness into the background and to bring into notice all the limpidity which the old poet, like some maker of glass, forced with mould and furnace upon his material. All know his rages, his coarseness, his arrogance, his noble admiration of manly qualities. Not so well known are his little flurries of tenderness, his adroitness in begging without whining, and his jolly joking at his own bulk. Out of it all he made beauty, though not the sort of beauty which we heirs of the romantics are most ready to look for and most prone to enjoy. And, in a way, his very failures in achieving his own sort of beauty do his fame a service. They show that the great galleon is too big for these bounded waters. They turn the mind to the plays, to the great comedies, in which he could move at large, and could turn his great poetic imagination to the making of his peculiar form of beauty.

THE MYSTERY OF YEATS

(1941)

'By the way, what *are* Keats?' asked the squire before taking
the chair at a lecture on the subject in the parish hall. Mr Louis
MacNeice's book [1] may well leave the reader asking, not by
the way but fundamentally, 'What *was* Yeats?' The question
is a tribute to Mr MacNeice's work. His subject was the
poetry of W. B. Yeats, and the reader's difficulty is to form
a clear image of the man who reveals himself in that poetry.
He will not ask for finality. A man can no more be static than
his poetry can be. Both represent a process of becoming. But
whereas in poetry even so gossamer, so 'elfin' (the word is
Lord David Cecil's) as Mr Walter de la Mare's, it is possible
to find the man that wrote it so that we can say, within limits,
what Mr de la Mare 'is', and 'is not', study of Yeats's poetry
yields not nearly so definite an idea of what Yeats 'was'.

Yeats is always eluding, Proteus-like, our grasp; showing
himself as now this, now that; now a pale and limp romantic,
now a bawdy and bloodthirsty realist; now a patriot-rebel and
now a scorner of all politics and national aspiration; now too
rare for human intercourse and now thick with the people;
searching now here, now there, in pagan legend, oriental
religion, Christian mysticism, spiritualism, the senses, for a
home which he never found. Like other very active intelli-
gences, he changed, naturally, as time went on; and chrono-
logy, which plays a large part in his poetry, can help to explain
his life. Here Mr Macneice's work is invaluable. A little
over-argumentatively perhaps, and not always in the directest
line to his point, he follows with subtlety and perception the
course, or courses, that Yeats followed from youth to old age.

[1] *The Poems of W. B. Yeats.* By Louis MacNeice. Oxford University
Press.

12

He makes every step as clear as it can be made. And in the end we are left feeling baffled and unsatisfied. What, after all, *was* Yeats? From other sources than his poetry we know that in practical affairs he was capable, business-like and masterful, a very clear-cut figure of a theatrical manager before and behind the curtain. But when Mr MacNeice has tracked him from this inspiration to that, from one influence to another, we find that we have been following the course of a man who never found himself, who, as each new path allured him, persuaded himself that now at last he was going the right way, only to be once more homeless. His superlatively swift and receptive mind could be easily allured but never convinced, though he could for a time mistake allurement for conviction. He found, therefore, no rest and no fulfilment. He eludes us to the end, because he was to the end eluded by himself. That would be no affair of ours if it were not for this: that no example or selection from his poetry, nor the whole *corpus* of his poetry, proclaims the whole man. It is as if all his poetry were but a preparation for the poetry that he was going to write when he had found himself.

In the difficult art of critical biography Mr MacNeice's book will win high honour. He has taken trouble to learn the conditions in which Yeats's poetic genius was bred, fostered and enlarged; and as a poet of a younger generation he can (and does) judge those conditions candidly, but without prejudice. He knows and speaks his own mind, but has more than enough historical sense to keep him from easy sneers at his forerunners. As an Irishman, too (and clearly it makes no difference that he comes from Northern Ireland), he has a sympathetic understanding of Yeats's attitude to Ireland and to England.

Starting, then, with the young Irishman not entirely at ease among his English fellows, he shows him as the disciple of Pater, of Morris, of Rossetti, the friend of Lionel Johnson and Ernest Dowson, 'hating rationalism and everyday realism', and persuading himself that poetry should have no truck with real and contemporary life. Of these aesthetic poets of the eighteen-nineties Mr MacNeice says: 'To most people of my generation their mentality seems more than foreign.' Foreign it was, and mainly French. 'More than foreign' can mean little except 'other than human'; and older generations will admit the futility of looking among the early poems of Yeats for the promise of great, human, English poetry to come. Not in *The Wanderings of Oisin*, long and elaborate though it is, are there signs of any substance under the decoration.

Some of the lyrics, it is true, are distinctive. *We who are old, old and gay*—the lovely dirge sung by the people of Faery over two mortal lovers—is prophetic in content, in the supple rhythms and in the straightforward diction; and of the very popular *Lake Isle of Innisfree*, which Mr MacNeice defends as a genuine expression of an experienced longing, Yeats himself said that it was 'my first lyric with anything in its rhythm of my own music'. Fortunately it escaped Yeats's itch to rewrite his poems, or it would no longer have begun with 'I will arise and go now', but with something that was not a 'conventional archaism'. When he tried ridding these early lyrics of their youthful characteristics, he did not always do them any good. Mr MacNeice takes as an example the poem which in 1892 (and in a slightly revised form in 1912) began: 'The quarrel of the sparrows in the eaves', and then (as it is printed in the *Collected Poems* of 1939) was rewritten throughout and begins with 'The brawling of a sparrow in the eaves'. In the new version, he admits, the lines are 'sonorous and bell-like', and the poem is 'no longer languid'. But

perhaps this poem ought to be languid. There is no law which demands that all poems should be close-knit or vigorous or virile. The poem is no longer languid but it no longer rings true.

There is sound advice there for the reader as well as for the poet. It is better to take these pretty things—and extraordinarily pretty some of them are—as we find them, and to admit that young Yeats was a languid and imitative aesthete, without Lionel Johnson's background of high learning or Dowson's inimitable poignancy.

We who are old, old and gay is there, all the same, to give a very broad hint that Yeats had something of his own to offer. At the back of his mind was Irish history and Irish myth. In his lifelong search for a settled background, he seems to have turned first to the stories and characters, the traditions and dreams of ancient Ireland. It was, in fact, only another device for turning his back on contemporary life and common humanity. He won from it great stores of new material, and much enlarged his range; but he did not genuinely believe in it all, as AE believed in it. It encouraged, therefore, Yeats's tendency to take refuge in symbolism. Mr MacNeice tells us that Yeats knew little at first hand of the poetry of Verlaine and Mallarmé; but Mr Arthur Symons was busy in those days bringing English readers acquainted with the French symbolists, and, if Yeats needed any such encouragement, there it was. In one of the most feline of his critical passages Mr MacNeice writes:

It was, Yeats goes on, 'with Goethe and Wordsworth and Browning that poetry gave up the right to consider all things in the world as a dictionary of types and symbols and began to call itself a critic of life and an interpreter of things as they are'. It is a good comment on the mentality of the nineties that it could think of poets like Homer or Chaucer or Villon as esoteric students poring over a dictionary of symbols.

Symbolism can be great fun for the symbolist poet and a source of mild entertainment to the select and leisured reader. But to all for whom poetry is not a game but a fundamental need it is a bore. Art is not 'liberated from life' by being made unintelligible; and any symbol the interpretation of which is known only to the few initiated is death, not to the despised common life, but to the poetry. Far from purifying it, such things corrupt it. Mr MacNeice anticipates the contention that 'Yeats's cat-headed figures or hounds with one red ear are no more *spiritual* than the everyday figures or objects met with in the Greek Anthology or in Burns or Wordsworth'. They are, indeed, or may easily become, less spiritual —mechanical contrivances for the expression of esoteric meaning at the expense of the exoteric meaning; and thus they obstruct the response of the spirit to the appeal of the poetry. Some of them, like a dog with one red ear, have the taint of the ridiculous which lurks in so many of the Irish legends. (Conchubar, we read in Yeats's note to *The Secret Rose*, had been struck by a ball made out of the dried brains of an enemy and hurled out of a sling; and this ball had been left in his head, and his head had been mended with thread of gold because his hair was like gold, and thus he lived for seven years.) Others are delightfully decorative:

> Their legs long, delicate and slender, aquamarine their eyes,
> Magical unicorns bear ladies on their backs.

It is to the good—to the good of us, the readers—that from these Irish myths Yeats should have drawn, especially in his earlier years, a set of values in which the dream life is truer than the waking life—values which may correct our too much absorption in the day-to-day material traffic of life. We may read the little poem of *Fergus and the Druid*, or *The Man who Dreamed of Faeryland*, or the crown of all this sort of work in Yeats, the play of *The Shadowy Waters*, and be spiritually the richer. But as Yeats's life-long search for his spiritual home went on and he added Oriental to Irish lore, and adventured into mysticism, into spiritualism, into astrology, into metaphysics, he acquired more and more symbols which appeared to him to be means of self-expression but were, in fact, devices for self-concealment. His human sympathies had begun to widen before Lady Gregory drew him into the popular atmosphere of the theatre; but to the very end he suffered from a sort of hang-over from the fastidious contempt for ordinary life that had kept him 'reclining on a yellow satin sofa' in his days of aesthetic languor.

> John Synge, I and Augusta Gregory, thought
> All that we did, all that we said or sang
> Must come from contact with the soil, from that
> Contact everything Antaeus-like grew strong.
> We three alone in modern times had brought
> Everything down to that sole test again,
> Dream of the noble and the beggar-man.

The Mystery of Yeats

The corollary, says Mr MacNeice, is that the aristocrats must be kept on their pedestals and that the peasants (which would include the beggar-man), 'finally, must remain where they have nothing to lose'. That is a sociological rather than a poetical concern (and the relation between poetry and sociology is a matter on which Mr MacNeice writes in another chapter with vigour and good sense); but, sociology apart, such a view of society is obviously arbitrary and artificial.

As Yeats matured, his symbols grew in dignity; his tower in particular is both noble and manifold. But the reader never feels safe. When certain poems obviously cannot mean just what they say (for the unicorns and the ladies are not only what they appear) any other poem may also mean something other than it says. A section of Yeats's poetry which grows upon the mind, perhaps, more than any other, *The Tower* of 1928, includes a poem of inexhaustible beauty and power, *Leda and the Swan*. On the face of it, it is a tremendous piece of description. It takes the breath away with the lines about the engendering of

> The broken wall, the burning roof and tower
> And Agamemnon dead;

and it ends with what looks like a capital example of a question that has occurred to many in a paler form. The women whom the poets loved—did they put on any of the poets' genius, or remain their earthly selves? And this woman—rapt into the embrace of the godhead—'Did she put on his knowledge with his power?' But that, we learn from Mr MacNeice, is not what Yeats meant. This poem, with other references to Leda,

signifies his belief that, in defiance of Aristotle, history has its roots in philosophy, that the eternal (Zeus) requires the temporal (Leda), further (for the myth is complex) that the human being (Leda) requires the animal (the swan), that God and Nature in fact require each other, and that the world will only make sense in terms of an incarnation.

Is not all this, we cry, taking us a long way from Poetry? When Yeats expounded in a prose work, *A Vision* (1925), the philosophy to which his cabbalistic and oriental studies had then brought him, he wrote, says Mr MacNeice, 'a book more unreadable than most orthodox philosophy'. Anything but unreadably, Mr MacNeice himself expounds the philosophy of Yeats. But in his Preface he had used a phrase which sticks in the mind even through the reading of his acute and learned book, and asserts itself with something like violence when the poems and the plays themselves are in hand or mind: 'I would repeat that a poem is about something but that a poem also *is*.'

> Come let us mock at the great
> That had such burdens on the mind
> And toiled so hard and late
> To leave some monument behind,
> Nor thought of the levelling wind.
>
> Come let us mock at the wise;
> With all those calendars whereon
> They fixed old aching eyes,
> They never saw how seasons run,
> And now but gape at the sun.
>
> Come let us mock at the good
> That fancied goodness might be gay,
> And sick of solitude
> Might proclaim a holiday:
> Wind shrieked—and where are they?
>
> Mock mockers after that
> That would not lift a hand maybe
> To help good, wise or great
> To bar that foul storm out, for we
> Traffic in mockery.

That is free from any marked search after what Mr Mac-Neice calls 'the bugbear of Beauty'. But anything more self-contained and self-sufficient, anything that more definitely *is* it would be hard to find. 'Things out of perfection sail', sings Old Tom in *Words for Music Perhaps*; and over and over again things seem to sail out of perfection into perfection on Yeats's pages. If it is true that he had no 'ear' and used to count the syllables on his fingers, the clearer it becomes that he wrote not with his brain alone. We are almost encouraged to believe in magic, when poem after poem exists by virtue of what Mr MacNeice would call truth, but others may be content to call beauty, seeing that beauty involves that essential truth to self. It matters not what the poems are about. We may declare now that there never was a poet who had made so much poetic truth about love-making; that he sings regret, defiance, dignity, impudence, reverence, gaiety, desire—a score of things, with a perfection denied to others. Nearly every poem is an individual joy.

Yet at the end of it all we come back to the original question —What *was* Yeats? He was not the languid aesthete. Was he the bawdy and bloodthirsty old man? Was he any other of the many whose voices are heard in these ever-alluring and ever-baffling pages? If, as must be true, he was all of them, he is still to seek. Perhaps he thought and strove too much to expound his changing vision of existence—wrote too much in prose to inquire, and explain, and explain away. In poetry he has left perfection; but he was still on the way to finding himself and integrating the warring elements in his mind and spirit.

MR DE LA MARE'S WORLD

(1942)

Thirty years ago, when Mr Walter de la Mare published the volume of his poems called *The Listeners*, *The Times Literary Supplement* said of him:

> There are some who have the gift of listening in quiet hours for a music that comes to them now and again when the noise of life is still. Mr de la Mare is one of these.... But besides listening he has the gift of hearing; not constantly, for in some of these poems the music is vague, as if his ears had strained after it in the distance and not quite caught it; but in others it is clear, as if he were a musician who had taken down the notes of a new chime of bells sounding from an unseen tower. For this music of his always seems to come from nowhere and to cease without giving any hint of its source.

What the critic said then (and experienced readers of this *Supplement* will easily recognize the touch of Arthur Clutton-Brock) is as true of the whole body of Mr de la Mare's poetry for adults, now first collected into one edition,[1] as it was of the volume of 1912, and of the volume of 1918, called *Motley*, our review of which added a shrewd observation—that readers of some, at least, of Mr de la Mare's poems find themselves 'still listening after the words are done'. If such criticism seems to make too little of the creative act of the *poietes*, it does so only in order to present an image that shall well express a distinctive characteristic in the results of that creative act. When Mr de la Mare is 'all out', when he is functioning to the full (and how Clutton-Brock would storm at us for the bare suggestion of a machine!), his poems show no more trace of any intellectual labour that may have gone to the making of them than do Blake's. His first book of poems (the new volume contains none of his 'rhymes primarily intended for

[1] *Collected Poems.* By Walter de la Mare. With decorations by Berthold Wolpe. Faber and Faber.

children', which therefore do not concern us here) included
The Death-Dream, which begins thus:

> Who now put dreams into thy slumbering mind?
> Who, with bright Fear's lean taper, crossed a hand
> Athwart its beam, and stooping, truth maligned,
> Spake so thy spirit speech should understand,
> And with a dread 'He's dead!' awaked a peal
> Of frenzied bells along the vacant ways
> Of thy poor earthly heart; waked thee to steal,
> Like dawn distraught upon unhappy days,
> To prove nought, nothing? Was it Time's large voice
> Out of the inscrutable future whispered so?

In 1906 that may have been much admired. To-day we smile
at the touching, though rather absurd, notion of Walter de la
Mare consciously labouring away at those rhymes and asso-
nances within the lines, at the alliteration, at all the glitter and
the ornament—a wedding-cake that has no cake inside. In
other poems in that volume, *Treachery*, for instance, and
Autumn, he showed another weakness of the too-conscientious
craftsman—too anxious a care for symmetry and balance; and
perhaps it only served the poet in him right that critics in those
days were ready to find them 'clumsy' and 'harsh' and (for
they went so far) 'lacking in charm'. When the poet in him
keeps the craftsman in his place, we may get something like
this *April Moon*:

> Roses are sweet to smell and see,
>   And lilies on the stem;
> But rarer, stranger buds there be,
>   And she was like to them.
>
> The little moon that April brings,
>   More lovely shade than light,
> That, setting, silvers lonely hills
>   Upon the verge of night—
>
> Close to the world of my poor heart
>   So stole she, still and clear;
> Now that she's gone, O dark, and dark,
>   The solitude, the fear.

('Wordsworth!' says the reader's involuntary association. And ten to one during the first stanza it had murmured 'Landor!' That is a point about Mr de la Mare's poetry that must be touched upon but need not take up much time. His singularity is almost complete; yet he is so firmly rooted in the tradition of English poetry that there is no great English poet—not even Meredith, or Hardy—who, at this line or that, may not flash across the reader's mind.)

April Moon first appeared in *Motley* (1918). In *The Listeners* (1912) there was a poem called *The Stranger*, the third stanza of which runs:

> There, when the dusk is falling,
>   Silence broods so deep
> It seems that every air that breathes
>   Sighs from the fields of sleep.

No craftsman-skill could produce that. It is poet-magic. We know all the words; we could speak all of the phrases in our ordinary conversation without making it any the less ordinary. It takes a poet to make old words new and turn sounds into stars. It is difficult to imagine Mr de la Mare listening for, hearing and taking down the music of *The Death-Dream*. As we read *April Moon* or *The Stranger*, and as we 'still listen after the words are done', it is more difficult to imagine him, wet towel on head and strong tea in hand, roughing the music out and polishing it up.

April Moon, his old admirers will say, is not a distinctive example of his poetry. Perhaps not; it might have been written by someone else. But we have quoted it in order to illustrate from poems lying outside his peculiar plot the difference which we believe to be the only difference between the poet of 1906 —the youngster at the same stage as Shakespeare in *Love's Labour's Lost*, delighting in words and in his own power over the wonderful things—and the mature poet who knew the dangers of that kind of self-assertion and was now wise enough to do what Clutton-Brock called listening. Before he grew up he had given evidence of other qualities, which need not detain us. From *The Listeners* the new book prints *Arabia*, which sings the pure song of romance; and next to it *The Tired Cupid*, which is only one of many poems showing his firm hold on detail. That is, perhaps, the best gift to be got from some of the longer and more laboured poems, such as *Goliath*, *Gloria Mundi*, or *Idleness*. They do at least show him possessed of the sensibility to detail and the power of precise statement which we welcome in all great poets, and miss when Shelley or Swinburne denies them to us. In the poetry of this listener, this dreamer, that precision of detail is bone and muscle, the sturdiest of guardians against the flabbiness and vagueness that too easily beset the dreamers.

For all that, not one of the early poems that we have quoted or mentioned lacks evidence of the mind, or perhaps rather the spirit, that created the distinctive work. To go back to the beginning, *The Death-Dream* has a characteristic title; and the lines that follow those we have quoted are these:

> Or but the horror of a little noise
> Earth wakes at dead of night? Or does Love know
> When his sweet wings weary and droop, and even
> In sleep cries audibly a shrill remorse?
> Or, haply, was it I who out of dream
> Stole but a little way where shadows course,
> Called back to thee across the eternal stream?

That 'sweet' in the third line is almost a signature. In *Keep Innocency*, another and a far more beautiful early poem to which events have restored its immediate poignancy, he writes of the 'sweet pomp' of old warfare which sweeps hurtling by before the eyes of childhood. But that goes for little compared with the dead of night, the horror, remorse, dream, shadows, all that shows the poet who finds night more real than day and dream more real than waking.

He has been at pains—we should like to say that he has condescended—to explain himself. In one poem he did so by means of a warning:

> Be not too wildly amorous of the far,
> Nor lure thy fantasy to its utmost scope.

Thus he writes at the beginning of *The Imagination's Pride*, and later comes:

> O brave adventure! Ay, at danger slake
> Thy thirst, lest life in thee should, sickening, quail:
> But not toward nightmare goad a mind awake,
> Nor to forbidden horizons bend thy sail—
> Seductive outskirts whence in trance prolonged
> Thy gaze, at stretch of what is sane-secure,
> Dreams out on steeps by shapes demoniac-thronged
> And vales wherein alone the dead endure.
>
> Nectarous those flowers, yet with venom sweet.
> Thick-juiced with poison hang those fruits that shine
> Where sick phantasmal moonbeams brood and beat,
> And dark imaginations ripe the vine.
> Bethink thee: every enticing league thou wend
> Beyond the mark where life its bound hath set
> Will lead thee at length where human pathways end
> And the dark enemy spreads his maddening net.

That way madness lies; but where, precisely, has life set its bound? What is 'life'? Where do human pathways end? The poet is only preserving his own balance; and his warning is only the other face of his courage and resolution. We may be forgiven for thinking of the skater who set forth upon the unsafe ice in order to see how far he could go without falling in. Mr de la Mare has kept to the very end of this book his reasoned and argued self-defence, the long poem called *Dreams*. He admits the dangers but he claims his right to his own kingdom of dreams, and with it the right of every man:

> O Poesy, of wellspring clear,
> Let no sad Science thee suborn,
> Who art thyself its planisphere!
> All knowledge is foredoomed, forlorn—
> Of inmost truth and wisdom shorn—
> Unless imagination brings
> Its skies wherein to use its wings.
>
> Two worlds have we: without; within:
> But all that sense can mete and span,
> Until it confirmation win
> From heart and soul, is death to man.

Of grace divine his life began;
And—Eden empty proved—in deep
Communion with his spirit in sleep

The Lord Jehovah of a dream
Bade him, past all desire, conceive
What should his solitude redeem;
And to his sunlit eyes, brought Eve.
Would that my day-wide mind could weave
Faint concept of the scene from whence
She awoke to Eden's innocence!

And the conclusion must be counted among the cardinal
utterances of the poets on the poetic faith:

When then in memory I look back
To childhood's visioned hours I see
What now my anxious soul doth lack
Is energy in peace to be
At one with nature's mystery:
And Conscience less my mind indicts
For idle days than dreamless nights.

We have given a great deal of space to poems by Mr de la
Mare which are not the purest waters of his genius   His
experienced admirers will forgive this, we hope, in view of the
current tendency to accuse him of running away from reality
and playing by himself with vain imaginings. His prose stories
rather than his poetry express his yearning 'for mortal glimpse
of death's immortal rose'; but the poems we have quoted show
that he is well aware of his own bent, and also completely
purposed to follow it. So far from running away from reality,
he adventures in search of it. It is for him, not for us, to say
which is reality to him, the world of sense or the world of
dream; and the proof, for us, can only lie in the literature that
comes of it. *Tom's Angel* is a straw that tells which way the
wind blows:

No one was in the fields,
   But me and Polly Flint,
When, like a giant across the grass,
   The flaming angel went.

But 'me' was not the only one who saw the angel. Polly Flint saw him first. His existence could have no surer proof than this matter-of-course assertion. The children were terrified. And, though it has not so much that is dreadful in its mystery as Mr de la Mare's stories have, the dream world of his poetry is no Bower of Bliss. It can be terrible. Courage, steadiness and faith are asked of any who would be at home in it. To explore it in search of the terror that lurks there would reveal a sickness of soul comparable only with that of the Suicide Club in *The New Arabian Nights*; and the doom of such morbidity would be either dumbness or inarticulate gibbering. Not so is poetry made. This listener makes his poetry because in all simplicity he listens to what is most real and most fundamental in his own soul, and he utters it not from the brain only but from the whole of his physical, mental and spiritual being:

> Sweet sounds, begone —
>   Whose music on my ear
> Stirs foolish discontent
>   Of lingering here;
> When, if I crossed
>   The crystal verge of death,
> Him I should see
>   Who these sounds murmureth.
>
> Sweet sounds, begone —
>   Ask not my heart to break
> Its bond of bravery for
>   Sweet quiet's sake;
> Lure not my feet
>   To leave the path they must
> Tread on, unfaltering,
>   Till I sleep in dust.
>
> Sweet sounds, begone!
>   Though silence brings apace
> Deadly disquiet
>   Of this homeless place;
> And all I love
>   In beauty cries to me,
> 'We but vain shadows
>   And reflections be.'

26

Mr de la Mare's World

That *Music Unheard* is followed immediately in the new book by the pitiful prayer of *The Dreamer*:

> Traitor to life, of life betrayed
> O, of thy mercy deep,
> A dream my all, the all I ask
> Is sleep.

Assuredly here is no coward courting of dreams for lust of sensation.

His own psychology, as we call it nowadays, the events and influences in his life which have made his dream world his real world, provide and will provide a very interesting study for the kind of literary criticism which looks upon the finished work chiefly for what it may tell about the inner history of the man who created it. No bad concomitant of such a study, possibly no bad introduction to it, is the contemplation (and happy he who could make it as 'impassioned' as the contemplation which Pater ascribed to Wordsworth) of the finished work, of the poetry as it appears in lines of black letters on white paper, thence passing through the eye to the ear and to the mind. Out of several qualities, one alone in Mr de la Mare's poetry would be enough to prove its complete and fundamental sincerity. Has any other poet so pervading a pathetic tone? There are singing voices which, with no intention in the singer, bring lumps into the throats of their hearers in music of which other voices may try and fail to express the sadness. Mr de la Mare is like a singer who has such a voice. He has always had it. When he is at his most genial—in *Jenny Wren*, for instance, and *Titmouse* and *The Robin*—it is an undertone in the purest of bell-notes. It is as constant in him as the sense of mystery, which trembles in a work of such exquisite delicacy as *The Moth*, shudders in *The Listeners* and *The Journey* and grows tremendous and awful in *The Image*:

> Hewn in that virgin rock, nude 'gainst the skies,
> Loomed mighty Shape—of granite brow and breast,
> Its huge hands folded on its sightless eyes,
> Its lips and feet immovably at rest.

27

Where now the wanderers who this image scored
For age-long idol here?—Death? Destiny? Fame?—
Mute, secret, dreadful, and by man adored;
Yet not a mark in the dust to tell its name?

More mysterious than Shelley's *Ozymandias*, that poem is perhaps less, yet more effectively mysterious than some other poems in the book, because the wonder is given a more concrete form than Mr de la Mare usually allows himself. It is true that readers of these poems who are less alert to the call of mystery than the poet himself (and few can hope to equal him in that alertness) will often be left wondering what he means; and sometimes, no doubt, they will be justified in ascribing their dissatisfaction to Mr de la Mare's failure to give this poem or that what has been called 'a recognizable prose anatomy of structure'. For the most part, his poetry asks of the reader a trustful surrender, a willingness to listen in the spirit in which the poet himself listens—like Joan of Arc—to voices from which he has no right to expect what his own mind can explain. From his trust in those voices, his determination not to lay craftsman hands upon material which is not the pure ore of his inmost being, come the consistency and the singularity which make his poetry unmistakably his own. And no honest reader can harbour the delusion that the reality of the dream-world seems to the poet to be any excuse for shirking responsibility in the waking world, or for being indifferent to its beauty. Rarely writing any but short and lyrical poems, Mr de la Mare has a variety that takes in such lucid simplicity as that of *The Fleeting*:

Alone in the muteness, lost and small,
I watched from far-off Leo fall
An ebbing trail of silvery dust,
And fade to naught; while, near and far,
Glittered in quiet star to star;
And dreamed, in midnight's dim immense,
Heaven's universal innocence.

O transient heart that yet can raise
To the unseen its pang of praise,
And from the founts in play above
Be freshed with that sweet love!

and takes in also strange, cloudy and terrible uncertainties; variety ranging from simple delight in natural beauty to spiritual joys and sorrows, hunger and ecstasy, for which genius only can find the words. He takes his reader through the screen of the artist into the larger and stranger world beyond, and gains his power to know the entrancing beauties of that world and to face the enormous terrors and uncertainties through which alone those beauties can be seen and known. And meanwhile the bells—'the new chime of bells sounding from an unseen tower'—ring for him, and so for us, overtones and undertones so many and so sweet that the ear can never be tired of listening to catch yet more of them, nor the spirit from rejoicing in the manifold life which they stir into action.

LEIGH HUNT AND HIS WORK

(1930)

To-day two old Bluecoat boys increase in honour. The younger of them, Mr Edmund Blunden, puts forth a book which may revive a drooping faith in the future of the art of biography.[1] It shows its subject whole and in the round, and not in two dimensions, dashingly sketched from the angle which most amuses the biographer. It proves that plenty of detail is not incompatible with free movement and grace of narrative; that selection need not mean suppression, nor distortion; that to make a character live in a book it is not necessary to give up trying to grapple with all the evidence, and that a good biographer can express the truth of himself in expressing the truth of his sitter. Mr Blunden's book is at once good narrative, good portraiture, and good criticism; and this is the more remarkable because his work upon it has been interrupted. The book appears years later than he intended, but it shows no signs of loss of grip or interest.

The other Bluecoat boy to be now honoured is the subject of the book, Leigh Hunt. The honour comes none too early; and when it comes it must begin by appearing to be rather the removal of reproach than positive praise. The immediate effect, at any rate, upon most readers will be to make them admit that Leigh Hunt was a better man and a better writer than they thought. Mr Brimley Johnson, Mr H. S. Milford, Mr S. E. Winbolt, Mr Blunden himself, have of recent years been drawing towards this rehabilitation; but it was nothing like complete until the publication of this 'careful' (it is Mr Blunden's word) biography. Except Charles Lamb and Thomas Barnes, all the men of the group to whom Leigh Hunt may be said to have belonged were in their time

[1] *Leigh Hunt: a Biography.* By Edmund Blunden. Cobden-Sanderson.

savagely and coarsely attacked. But the fame of Shelley, Keats, Coleridge, even the turbulent and trouble-seeking Hazlitt, have all outsoared the shadow of the old contempt and fury, leaving poor Hunt still groping in it. Perhaps if we could come to understand why he was even worse abused than the others by some of his contemporaries we should begin to understand also why it has taken him so much longer to find his Blunden and to be honoured as he deserves.

The secret, we suspect, lay in a shortcoming of Hunt's own mind and character. Whether we call it, with Mr Saintsbury, triviality, or give it kinder words such as lightness or vagueness, it brought upon him, almost naturally, a punishment greater than he deserved. There was nothing in him to match the quality of greatness, the aristocracy of intellect and soul, which put Shelley out of reach of the most obtuse and brutal of his enemies; and Keats's achievement no less than Keats's death called the pack off. Hunt had not their panoply; and his vulnerability was all the plainer because life began by treating him well and went on to treat him rather scurvily. At school he had more pocket-money, more easy social talent and more comfortable friends than the others. His showy, expansive father published the boy's childish poems, with the names of many grand friends among the subscribers; and when the youth had lived that down, there opened to him the combined shelter and stimulus of his brother John. It would be difficult to admire John Hunt more than he deserved. In his solid English way this half-English champion of truth and good will was of the salt of the earth. But the less articulate he was himself and the more quietly he stuck, without care for praise or blame, to his opinions, the more opportunity he gave to his younger brother to think himself a great fellow, since it was he who had the words. The words he undoubtedly had. To read again those early papers in *The Examiner* is to believe that all which Leigh Hunt lacked to be supreme in that kind was a touch of the deadly quiet of a French wit, of, say Paul Louis Courier; and the poems of 'Harry Brown', the 'Non mi ricordo' poem on Queen Caroline's trial and the other political verses are brilliantly clever. The famous passage about the Prince Regent was worth going to prison for: there is still a heady joy to be had in reading it.

But prison was bad for Leigh Hunt in the very way in which it might have been expected not to be. It did not deepen him, make him more serious, plough his spirit to fruitfulness. His mind was innocent, though it was sharp, and fairly quiet, though it was lively; but it did not take stone walls and iron bars for a hermitage. It took them for a bower, a parlour. It painted them up into a pretty background against which 'Libertas' might display his charming, gallant self. And Charles and Mary Lamb, with their devotion, and Byron, with his eagerness to take the chance of posing as a friend of freedom and a lover of letters with no snobbery about him, added to the prisoner's temptation to be an interesting hero. What happened when he came out of prison was what seems to modern minds inevitable. His health was weakened. His mind was unaccustomed to contact with the untidy, noisy muddle of the great outer world. He was no longer the centre of a little secluded stage. He suffered, acutely at first, from fear of the crowd. He shrunk away farther than before from reality. What his son long afterwards called his 'very precarious grasp of mere dry facts' became then more precarious than it would have been without those two years of shelter in the prison-bowers. If it had been only his grasp of such mere dry facts as that half-a-crown and a shilling make three-and-sixpence (which he positively did not know), it would not have mattered much.

But the vagueness went farther and deeper than that. It invaded his vision of all life: it invaded his practice of prose and poetry: it made him, through its appendages of affection and of a sloppy benevolence, an easy prey to the scoffer. Recent years have shown anew that there is no one quite so exasperating to men in general as he who preaches the gospel of joy, the power of good will, the force of the idea. To be tolerable to common opinion he must have behind him the authority, the sanction, the excuse, of an organized religion, or he must have a brain equal to meeting and defeating the sharpest onslaughts of the 'practical', the 'hard-headed', and the rest. Leigh Hunt had neither. His vague Deism infuriated the orthodox and left the rationalists (as we should call them now) dissatisfied; and his vague benevolence—even at its finest moment of expression, in *Captain Sword and Captain Pen*— was not quite stripped of the woolly wrapping which protected it against hard fact, keen sword-points and Scottish bludgeons. Hunt, witty, charming, learned, would talk for hours on end with his intellectual equals and superiors; yet mentally, as well as physically, he was always wrapped in his famous flowered dressing-gown (it is a pity that Mr Rex Whistler's amusing drawing on the wrapper of this very attractive Cambridge Press book should put him in a coat, instead of the garment which he must have worn in prison no less than in the Vale of Health). He never, so to speak, stripped and got down to it— to contact with the reality of his relation with men and things. Hence all that was deplorable in the uncertainty of his be-haviour to and about Byron, a story which Mr Blunden sets down with complete candour and generosity. And last, the vagueness lies at the root of the wretched business of Harold Skimpole, where Dickens's high spirits were responsible for a very large part of the shadow from which Leigh Hunt's character is only now emerging. The worst detail in that reproach—the most superficial, perhaps, but the most damaging in the general opinion—Mr Blunden now removes. Leigh Hunt was not a sponger. He was careless about money; but when it is generally known that his wife was not only im-practical but a tippler and a borrower, and that his son John was a fraudulent parasite on his father's friends, it will be admitted that Leigh Hunt himself behaved in these things not ignobly but nobly.

The time is not far off (perhaps it will come with the appearance of that reprint of Hunt's prose which many desire and no one seems inclined to undertake) when his readers will wonder how the reproach of being idle and irresponsible could ever have been attached to one whose life was a long series of fresh starts, new efforts, original experiments. Again, the lightness, the vagueness of his mind, partly no doubt innate and partly induced by circumstance, is the cause. Everybody knows that it is impossible to read two pages of Leigh Hunt, whether in prose or verse, without being made to shudder by some sudden, deplorable, unnecessary, inexplicable lapse from good sense or good taste. The collection of examples is too easy a game to be worth playing; but there are instances so surprising as to raise a doubt whether this very clever man was always master of his faculties. Even in the famous *Indicator* paper on angling he ruins, or at least snaps short, a brilliant piece of irony by a silly suggestion about wet feet and cut ankles. Notoriously, it is dangerous for him to think of a woman; and any idea of sensuous pleasure may make him almost unbearably luscious. He is a champion of joy, of the beauty of the world. He was himself cheerful and happy in circumstances which gave every cause for moroseness. Yet he is never so likely to become unpalatable as when he is being gay. It is especially dangerous for him to be facetious and flowery—to 'show off', with no matter what desire to charm. To modern readers the danger seems all the greater because of Hunt's fidelity to the convention of the journalistic 'we'. Suppose that a man is bent on talking about himself, and suppose that it is not in fact a very interesting subject, the natural egotism of a writer seems in him all the more obtrusive when he berobes and bewigs it with the first person plural. Hunt at his most affected and trivial—the Hunt, for example, of the introduction to *A Jar of Honey*—would be less irritating if, risking the appearance and denying himself the substance of egotism, he had boldly said 'I' or 'me'. Still, the lapses would have remained. And the reader wondering why it is that Hazlitt, for all his whimsies, his rudeness, his violations of good taste, never shocks as Leigh Hunt shocks, must remember Hunt's abstraction from reality, his want of grip upon facts, his preoccupation with his own luxuriant bowers of dreams and of feeling.

34

Leigh Hunt and His Work

Unfortunately for Hunt's fame to-day, his lusciousness, his vagueness, his rather sloppy benevolence are the very qualities likely to be most distasteful to the present age, which is busy in hammering as new a music and forging as new a beauty as may be out of the hardest and ugliest material it can find. And the younger readers are little likely to be drawn to him by his achievement in the history of literature. A history of literature there is, and in the making of it certain men have done certain things—to say which is not to say that those things could not have happened without them, but that in fact they did not. And among those men Leigh Hunt holds a more important place than his own achievement in writing would suggest. Let us follow the guidance of Mr Saintsbury, a great historian, as well as a great critic, of literature, and one who can hardly be suspected of having even, like Macaulay, 'a kindness' for Leigh Hunt. In the *Cambridge History of English Literature* Mr Saintsbury says of Hunt that 'he had, beyond doubt, the credit of being the first deliberately to desert the stopped decasyllabic couplet which had reigned over the whole eighteenth century and the latter part of the seventeenth'; and that, besides its versification, his *Rimini* gives other 'patterning' to easy verse narrative. In criticism Hunt 'had the merit of a most unusual and, at the same time, almost unique catholicity'. And in journalism:

to no single man is the praise of having transformed the eighteenth-century magazine, or collection of light miscellaneous essays, into its subsequent form due so much as to Hunt....Without Hunt, *Sketches by Boz* would have been a kind of Melchisedec, and *Household Words* improbable. His very enemies in *Blackwood* owed him royalty a hundred years ago, and it is doubtful whether even the most infallible and self-reliant youth of the twentieth century, when it writes articles of the 'middle' style, and even, sometimes, of the purely critical, is not similarly, though less directly, indebted to Hunt.

Of those tributes there is one on which it is especially pleasant to dwell. As critic, Leigh Hunt not only saw in Elizabethan drama things which had escaped even Lamb; he not only anticipated the young twentieth century in its interest in the

Restoration drama; he not only created the new dramatic criticism which, taken up by Hazlitt, grew to be one of the best works of the century. He it was who saw first the worth of Shelley and of Keats, who championed them as stoutly as he criticized them wisely, and did more than any other to force the recognition of their genius on a reluctant world. It may be true that *Rimini* and Hunt in general were a danger to fledgling Keats. That can count for nothing against what Hunt's judgement, courage and persistence did for the then new English poetry.

All this, however, may seem no reason for reading Leigh Hunt nowadays. Good reason, nevertheless, is not hard to find. And first of all might be suggested to adventurous spirits the fun that may result from his very uncertainty. Hunt lacked grip on the world and on his own thoughts and feelings. He 'sat at the receipt of impressions, rather than commanded them'. He did not progress; he fluttered. And, since his very lack of responsibility added to his natural fearlessness, he fluttered often into error. But he fluttered nearly as often into beauties which staider minds might miss. Mr Blunden speaks in a happy phrase of his 'twinkling sprightliness'. That and the constant freshness of his innocent feeling enable him to bring forth every now and then a very delightful thing. Of the song, 'Care Charming Sleep', in *Valentinian* he writes: 'How earnest and prayer-like are these pauses!' Of the deaths of little children: 'Those who have lost an infant are never, as it were, without an infant child.' Of Izaak Walton's appearance: 'He looks like a pike, dressed in broadcloth instead of butter.' It is well worth being shocked now and then for the sake of many a little felicity like these. And to read again in Hunt in the spirit which Mr Blunden's book induces is to find a larger amount of steady, good writing than was anticipated. There are things almost nauseating in *Rimini*; but it moves forward, it glows, it is full of life. Not only to an age grown tired of Pope is there joy in the metrical dancing and galloping of *The Palfrey*. *Ultra-crepidarius*, the satire on William Gifford, has some fine invective in it as well as some sloppy nonsense. The popular *Abou Ben Adhem*, the sonnet to Barnes and at least one of those to Hampstead, the verses on his sick child, and *Jenny kissed me*—to turn the pages of Mr Milford's collected edition of the poems (by no means forgetting *A Legend of Florence*) is to find good grounds for wishing that Leigh Hunt could have kept to poetry and have worked hard at it—harder than he suggests in his vision of bliss, 'reading romantic adventures and versifying the best of them'. His translations are supple and lively, though he was not always so careful of the meaning of his original as he and Mr Blunden imagine. But prose it had to be; and he was forced to know that his best prose was better than his best poetry.

It was best of all when he was trying to share his delight in other people's poetry. Except for his impatience with Pope and his utter inability to understand Dante (or even to abstain from a trivial impudence about him), he is a very good guide. In 'Imagination and Taste', so soon as he has got through a page or two of the kind of general reflection which Coleridge and Shelley—and even Watts-Dunton—have done much better, he proves himself not only a keen, sound critic, but an inspiring companion; and few are too well-read to be able to benefit by this bookman's passion for all sorts of books. And still there remain the *Autobiography*, in which he could talk about himself with more ease, earnestness and responsibility than elsewhere, and made one of the best books of that kind; the occasional essays on all subjects under the sun, in which his pleasantness, his grace, his 'twinkling sprightliness' atone for much that is shallow and vague and affected; and, best of all, such books as *An Old Court Suburb*, and *The Town*, in which, steadied by the facts of history, he may flutter away into fancy and back again with an ease in transition that none but himself could equal. In the end, perhaps, one is left feeling rather sad. Hunt's ability was extraordinary. He ought to have done better with it. But we may be proud of him, after all, for having done what he did under the conditions in which he lived and worked.

ANTHONY TROLLOPE

(1927)

Of recent years there have been growing signs that the fame
of Anthony Trollope's novels is emerging from the valley of
the shadow. It had passed through a very deep and dark part
of that valley, deeper and darker than that of any eminent
Victorian writer, except perhaps Tennyson. Now, the publication of Mr Michael Sadleir's biographical commentary; of
Miss Irwin's bibliography, which is a good guide to Trollope;
of a new and finely printed edition of *The Warden*, with new
illustrations by Mrs Ethel Gabain; and of a new addition to
the Trollopes in the *World's Classics*,[1] proves that at least
Trollope's head has come up into the light again.

But converts are ever suspect to those of the old faith.
A few stalwarts, among whom were both avowed men of
letters and private readers, have clung to Trollope through
everything. If Trollope is to be openly admired again, if those
who come new to him are going to say good things of him and
to be proud, instead of ashamed, to be his adherents, then those
of the old faith will want to know on what terms he is to be
received among them. There is a little craze abroad for Victorian colours and decoration. The faithful will be by no
means pleased if Anthony Trollope is admired, like a mound
of wax flowers or a loud piece of Berlin woolwork, because
he is 'quaint' and Victorian. Fielding is not admired because
he is eighteenth-century, nor Balzac because he is early nineteenth. The faithful will demand that Trollope's date and his
success in representing the spirit of his own time shall be, not,

---

[1] *Trollope: a Commentary*. By Michael Sadleir. Constable. *Anthony Trollope: a Bibliography*. By Mary Leslie Irwin. New York: The H. W. Wilson Company. *The Warden*. By Anthony Trollope. Elkin Mathews and Marrot. *Framley Parsonage*. By Anthony Trollope. The *World's Classics*. Milford.

of course, left out of count, but allowed no more than their due weight in the scales. If Trollope is to be admired only because he is typically Victorian, then Trollope will be misjudged and undervalued. Believe him to be, in however small a way, a good novelist, not of an age, and the faithful will be satisfied. On that account it is even more necessary for them than for those who are not of the old Trollopian faith to read Mr Sadleir's book with care—lest they should feel tempted to quote from *The Three Clerks* the phrase about 'the roguery of the Sadleirs'. No reader of Mr Michael Sadleir's novel *Privilege* needs to be reminded that he has a sense of period. He begins his study of Trollope with a study of Trollope's period; and in the first paragraph of his chapter on Trollope's books he writes:

His novels are so intimately interwoven with the social life of their period, are so much more obviously remarkable for their expression of period-psychology than for their literary texture, that their effect on posterity seems—and very curiously—to have varied according to the social rather than the literary preoccupations of those who read them.

And throughout the book he is so careful to keep in mind the qualities of the Mid-Victorian era and Trollope's grasp of them that he might easily give a careless or a prejudiced reader the idea that he, too, thinks Trollope to be all period. He is very far from thinking so. He is too sensitive a critic and too honest a thinker to harbour any such delusion. He has seen the whole of Trollope, and he does justice to it in this admirable study, which gives to old Trollopians new facts and documents, and to all a just and well-informed study of the man and of his work.

The conventions of his time are strong, it is true, in Trollope; and Mr Sadleir is probably right in thinking that his superficial acceptance of them is one of the greatest stumbling-blocks to readers of a later date. The strongest of all is the convention about gentility. Trollope has been accused of 'a nose for gentility'. To him a gentleman or a lady did, to a great extent, mean one born into the upper middle class. The peerage does not fret him, as it fretted Thackeray. He merely takes it jovially for granted that to be in the peerage is to be a knave or a fool, a cat or a vampire. There are a few exceptions—among them Plantagenet Palliser and the queer old farmer, Lord De Guest; and he could relent, as he relented between the Lady Julia of *The Small House at Allington*, in which she is described as disagreeable for no reason except that she had a title, and the Lady Julia of the *Last Chronicle of Barset*. But the greatest cad in all his novels is Lord Brotherton, whom the Dean of Brotherton threw into the fireplace; and the Germain and the De Courcy families represent Trollope's general attitude to the peerage. Of the 'lower orders', as his time called them, he has little to say, and that usually uncivil. To this generalization also there must be, in so vast a field, exceptions; but Trollope had none of Dickens's delight in the humours of the uneducated, and very little of Mr Hardy's admiration for their dignity. He will go out of his way, for instance, to tell us that Mrs Val's servants were at the beer-shop instead of walking her horses about. It was the general feeling of his time, and it lasted on into the novels of Meredith. But the people whom Trollope most disliked were those of indeterminate social position, or those who tried to attain a position above that in which they were born. He would not have written as contemptuously as he did about poor Norah Geraghty if she had not been trying to catch young Charley Tudor, nor of Amelia Roper if she had not been setting snares for Johnny Eames. They were gentlemen (for we are convinced, with Mr Sadleir, that Trollope put Johnny in that social category). Mr Slope (about whose person, by the way, Mr Sadleir's readers may learn some details which Trollope, under pressure, toned down before the book was published) was, of course, underbred: a slimy fellow trying to worm himself into places too high for him. No wonder Mrs Bold boxed his ears. And the true reason of Trollope's hatred of Adolphus Crosbie is not so much that he jilted Trollope's best-loved heroine, as that he, a gentleman born, tried, not for love nor even for true ambition but from mere snobbery, to wriggle up into a higher social plane. Alaric

Tudor was no snob; his 'Excelsior' did not include social climbing, and Undy Scott had no need to use that bait. And although, to sober judgement, young Phineas Finn behaved almost as badly to his lady-loves as did Crosbie, Trollope never hated Phineas. Phineas was poor and ambitious, but Phineas was always a gentleman.

It is the Mid-Victorian period speaking roundly, heartily, confidently: the voice of an upper middle class which thought little of a nobility barely yet convalescent from a surfeit of privilege and self-indulgence, but a middle class which serenely knew itself to be 'upper', and to exclude the Slopes and the Slides. It seems, indeed, very old fashioned nowadays; but, granting that, so far as it goes, it 'dates' Trollope, we must ask, first, what sort of gentleman and of lady Trollope, starting from these conventions, contrived to present. One need not be an out-and-out Trollopian to admit that of all the English novelists none (unless it were Jane Austen) could equal Trollope at drawing quietly well-bred people. A hundred instances might be given, but a single one will suffice:

'My dear Crawley,' the Archdeacon said,—for of late there seems to have grown up in the world a habit of greater familiarity than that which I think did prevail when last I moved much among men;— 'my dear Crawley, I have enough for both.' 'I would we stood on more equal grounds,' I said. Then as he answered me, he rose from his chair. 'We stand', said he, 'on the only perfect level on which such men can meet each other. We are both gentlemen.' 'Sir,' I said, rising also, 'from the bottom of my heart, I agree with you. I would not have spoken such words; but coming from you who are rich to me who am poor, they are honourable to the one and comfortable to the other.'

The truth of it cannot be escaped. Polished, autocratic, wealthy, worldly Archdeacon Grantly is face to face with uncouth, self-conscious, poor, unsuccessful Mr Crawley, who, though he has got a new coat and a cleared character, has not yet won free from the dominion of his old shabbiness and disgrace. Each recognizes in the other a quality which may be roughly described as breeding, but which includes something much greater than gentle birth and other than good form.

Then follows a further question. Admitting that Trollope accepted the social order of his time with all its conventions, does he therefore approve of all its consequences and implications? The answer is that he approves and disapproves exactly as his own common sense bids him. Mr Sadleir sees the novels as

almost without exception novels of a conflict between individual decencies and social disingenuities. And they are thus because he regarded private persons with a friendly optimism but society with cynical distrust.

Yet no English novelist, not even Fielding, was less of a reformer than Trollope. True, he can write with almost Peacockian shrewdness about an Internal Navigation Office, but he writes no less shrewdly about competitive examination. It would be hard to pin him down in the political novels to any definite opinion: vaguely liberal is as near as we can go to classify him. The preface to *The Vicar of Bullhampton* and some passages in that admirable story show him, again, in a reforming spirit; but what did he think of the agitation which caused Mr Harding to resign the Wardenship of Hiram's Hospital? The cynical distrust of society, of which Mr Sadleir writes, did not make him a reformer as Dickens was a reformer, nor a philosopher either such as George Eliot openly was or such as Mr Hardy has often denied that he is. Even his adored Thackeray is more critical of the social order and of the moral convention than was Trollope.

Since, then, this prolific author is neither a Victorian curio nor one who can delight the neo-Georgians by showing up the faults of the Victorians, on what plea shall those who do not yet know his books be lured into beginning them? There is only one that will hold water. Trollope was a novelist: he told most uncommon good stories. After all, telling good stories is the first duty of a novelist. But no sooner is the claim stated than it is necessary to begin whittling away occasions of contradiction. We have already quoted Mr Sadleir's opinion that the novels are 'much more remarkable for their expression of period-psychology than for their literary texture'; and Mr Sadleir may be right. The eighteen-eighties did very much to drive Trollope's fame down into the valley of the shadow, because it was then—just when younger English writers made an idol of Flaubert, grunting and sweating under the fardel of the *mot juste*, and Stevenson was bringing preciousness into fashion—that Trollope's posthumously published autobiography displayed him as a commercial author, with more care for royalties than for rhythms. Even the faithful were shaken; and the uninitiate were not likely to take the trouble to learn that some cause, which was probably Trollope's artistic modesty, had distorted the truth. Trollope wrote as he hunted, straight and fast. He was thinking all the time not of his words and his cadences but of his story and his people. He took, as Mr Sadleir can show, much trouble over some of his plots, and even then some of them would turn out untidy and ill-knitted. It was not (at any rate after his first attempts) that he had axes to grind and would violate probability in order to put an edge on them: it was that his imagination sometimes could see no farther ahead in his story than his short-sighted eyes could see in a run. To read any novel by Mr Hardy and to observe how much the story gains from the masterly descriptions, be they minute or heroic in scale, of forest, heath, town or meadow, by the poet's hand, is to fall to thinking how much richness, colour, and significance Trollope's stories lack because a little feeling for a house and a garden was his only susceptibility to the outward scene. Mr Sadleir does his duty by those who like to study the topography of Barsetshire, and he prints Trollope's own map; but one might as profitably attempt to identify the places visited by the hunters of the Snark as look for Barsetshire on the ordnance map. Trollope knew every house and field in it; but all that his readers know and all we need to know is that it is England. Of settings of other kinds—the Church, the law, politics (except Disraeli, does any novelist make politics so real and so interesting as Trollope?) he writes, not without mistakes, say the experts, but with fundamental truth; the spirit of place he leaves us to take for granted. And then—to continue the list of reservations—there are Trollope's many repetitions, and his many little discrepancies, his tiresome made-up names for minor characters, Neverbend, Hardlines, Holdenough, and so forth (Thackeray and his house of Sheepshanks were probably responsible for that); and even his love of old friends, which causes such meaningless interruptions as Crosbie's visit to the Hospital with Mr Harding.

There are plenty of faults, and there is not one which he cannot overcome when he likes. Half a page of Meredith or of *Treasure Island* may be richer in pleasure to the literary epicure than a whole volume of Trollope; but, though Trollope's prose may lack fineness, it lacks also affectation and self-consciousness. One small point worth noting is that it never has such falls as those which permitted Stevenson to call Scott an idle child. Another and a much greater thing is that for page after page Trollope goes on steadily doing his business, which was to tell his story; and for telling stories this honest, lively, vigorous prose of his is the best of means. Now and then, too, it can hit hard or flash with mischief: 'As for Mrs Proudie, our prayers for her are that she may live for ever'— it is so quietly popped in that a second or two may pass before the reader catches his breath at the full force of it.

He had written a book which had been characterized as tending to infidelity, and had more than once been invited to state dogmatically what was his own belief. He had never quite done so, and had then been made a dean.

It would be absurd to say that the man who wrote that last sentence was a clumsy or a dull writer. His letters show that there was more in him of that spirit than he cared to set free in his novels—being a little nervous, perhaps, of that very Victorian public which was sometimes found, or invented, as a rod for the chastening of this ebullient and not so very Victorian author. Some of his plots are, indeed, untidy and loosely knitted; but it would be hard to find in English fiction a story better contrived and more adroitly worked out than

44

Is he Popenjoy? The steps by which the differences between Lord and Lady George Germain are increased, and the delicately complicated relations between Lord George and his elder brother are the work of no bungler nor slave of the circulating library. And there is no denying him a mastery in the narration of the scenes that are definite as hill-tops in his sometimes straggling plans. One thinks of Carry Brattle's return home and of her forgiveness by her father; and one does not think of her unmoved. In a single novel Trollope shows Mrs Proudie twice set down before the Bishop's face, first by Mr Crawley, then by Dr Tempest. The occasions are much alike: the differences are cardinal. Each is in itself an excellent piece of story-telling: to study both is to see why it was the second, not the first, which broke the Bishop and ended the dominion of his wife. Here let us quote another example of Trollope at his best. There is no excitement in the scene. All that has happened is that Lord Chiltern, the wild son and heir, has at length come to see his father the Earl. They have had a pleasant little chat, and Lord Chiltern is about to leave the room:

'Stop half a moment, Oswald,' said the Earl. And then Lord Brentford did make something of a shambling speech, in which he expressed a hope that they two might for the future live together on friendly terms, forgetting the past. He ought to have been prepared for the occasion, and the speech was poor and shambling. But I think that it was more useful than it might have been, had it been uttered roundly and with that paternal and almost majestic effect which he would have achieved had he been thoroughly prepared. But the roundness and the majesty would have gone against the grain with his son, and there would have been a danger of some outbreak. As it was, Lord Chiltern smiled, and muttered some word about things being 'all right', and then made his way out of the room. 'That's a great deal better than I had hoped,' he said to himself; 'and it has all come from my going in without being announced.' But there was still a fear upon him that his father even yet might prepare a speech, and speak it to the great peril of their mutual comfort.

It is exact to the two men; and the quiet comedy of it is rich in the universal truth of fathers and sons.

Not prose, then, nor plot, nor description, nor even narrative is the element in story-telling for which the faithful have cherished Trollope. But he must be pretty good at them all, or he would have no means of expression for that at which he is very good indeed. And that is, making people. Making is, of Trollope, the only word for it. It is not drawing, because, of all novelists, he shows his people 'in the round': he dared to show Archdeacon Grantly night-capped, in the marital couch, like any Mr Caudle. It is not carving, because his people live and move and grow; and a grubby, drunken little Charley Tudor can develop into the happy husband and father and successful novelist. It is not presenting, because Trollope explicitly and sincerely disclaims (except when he is laboriously joking) any hand in it all: he has no story-teller's tricks, of mystification and the like; he never appears as the showman, and when he apostrophizes in the second person singular he only deepens the impression that he is watching, not directing. And therein lies the reason why some of his plots are untidy. The characters became so real that they went and did things for which he was not prepared. He is not, again, what modern criticism would call a psychological novelist (although, as Mr Sadleir shows in an appendix, several of his novels might be classed as psychological analyses), because he very rarely tries to make a character that would have been called abnormal in days before we all began to wonder whether any character was normal. But he can do it when he tries. We must give up the Signora Vesey Neroni. Some, even of the faithful, would admit that the Signora Vesey Neroni will not do, and that Mr Arabin, for all his inexperience in women, would have turned from her humbugging at a glance. Yet Mr Crawley was so abnormal as to be at one time nearly insane; and at least one discerning lover of Trollope has been tempted to think that only by accident did our 'humdrum' novelist carry Mr Crawley through with masterly consistency and truth. Perhaps the character of Chiltern, another very odd fellow in his way, whose making demanded equal power, though not in equal degree, may help to show that Mr Crawley was no accident. And, indeed, we are tempted to ask whether it is truly more difficult to make a Mr Crawley than to make any of the normal people as Trollope made them, by scores, and all within those narrow limits. One may fancy that, what with *The Warden* and *Barchester Towers*, one knows Mr Harding; and then in the *Last Chronicle*, when he is very old, comes the finishing touch:

> Nobody was milder in his dislikings than Mr Harding; but there were ladies in Barchester upon whose arm he would always decline to lean, bowing courteously as he did so, and saying a word or two of constrained civility.

That is a good example of the 'sure-footed subtlety' which endears Trollope to the faithful. Thus he makes his people. And he makes them so thoroughly that, though some are much more alive than others, it is very seldom that one has to ask such a question as whether Phineas Finn would really have been such an innocent ass as to tell Lady Laura about his love for Miss Effingham. Of these people there are hundreds; and, at any rate in the novels that are up to Trollope's average, no two are the same under different names. He has a few types which he likes to introduce. The successful, worldly ecclesiastic is one of them. A stranger seeing Archdeacon Grantly and Dean Lovelace at a big party might think them very much alike; Trollope knows precisely the difference between the silk purse and the sow's ear, for all the cunning workmanship. There are several young men who are weak about women; but no one is likely to confuse Phineas Finn, Adolphus Crosbie, Johnny Eames and Charley Tudor. Dull and pompous husbands are not few; but Mr Kennedy is not Lord George Germain; and when Major Grantly has been married for a few years to Grace Crawley he will be dull and pompous, but not like either of the others. And then there are the high-spirited girls, with a way of saying things which their time thought rather daring. Lily Dale and Violet Effingham are the best of them, but Lily is no more Violet than Madalina Demolines is Katie Woodward. It is best to bring Katie into the open, curls, consumption and all, and stand the racket. At her, if at any of Trollope's characters, the younger generation will hoot. Isolated, she may taste like yew-berries, or like barley-water 'unlaced'. But she must be seen compassed about with scores of her Trollopian sisters (let us not forget Marie Bromar in that most charming of the shorter stories, *The Golden Lion of Granpere*) of all degrees of sharpness and strength, of wit and of simplicity, but all endowed with certain qualities of sincerity, of courage in love, of gentleness, of dearness, which not only in the Victorian era were the privilege of womanhood.

Claverings, Greshams, Woodwards, Dales, Robartses, Proudies, Grantlys—they come crowding in hundreds before the mind—almost, as it seems, before the bodily eyes—of one who sits down to think over Trollope. The making of them was his great achievement, and the matter also of the great labour which this reputed careless writer put into his novels. The common stuff of human nature fascinated him; and he had an extraordinary perception of its variety and its interest. The plain humanity of his people is part of the reason why, more than the characters of any other novelist, they seem to be what is called real; and they become so real and so familiar that it is impossible for a moment to mistake them for incarnations of the tendencies and conventions of a period. They lived in the Mid-Victorian era; but they live in the human nature of all time.

He wrote in his own way; he drank huge draughts of English home-brewed from his own enormous tankard. If the glass had been smaller the contents might have been choicer, might have been wine of the high imagination, the very hippocrene. Trollope, never wholly free of his boyhood's uncouth miseries, did not believe himself fit to aim so high. 'My mechanical stuff', he calls it with no false modesty; and to wonder what he might have done had he concentrated his powers on trying how high rather than how fast and far he could fly is to ask for a Trollope who would be someone else than the known and well-loved Anthony. As Sir Arthur Quiller-Couch puts it, the prodigious quantity of his work is felt to be a quality: as the *Arabian Nights* would put it, his height was knocked into his width. But there is no saying whether less width would have meant greater height. To-day we are far enough away from his moment to shut our eyes without compunction to many of his lower flights. And when those are forgotten, it will be known that the engine of his best mechanical stuff was in truth the wings of a thoroughbred English weight-carrier named Pegasus.

SOME STORY-TELLERS

(1928)

A new collected edition of the tales of one modern story-teller, a new posthumous book by another, whose works were collected as long as seventeen years ago, and a new edition of selected works by the first great English master of story-telling[1] may well appeal to minds already attuned by the holiday spirit to the simpler forms of fiction. The two moderns are likely to set middle-aged men summoning up remembrance of some literary history of their youth. As they saw it then (and they probably saw it justly) the turn, or the fun (for these terms suit it much better than anything grander) began with *Treasure Island*, which was issued as a book in 1883. *Treasure Island* had treasures for two different kinds of seekers. Some pored over the exquisite workmanship, and quoted reverently its most precious phrases. Others revelled in a rattling good yarn. A strange thing had happened. A story-teller had written a rattling good yarn in beautiful English. The effect was instantly to put the rattling good yarn in a more favourable light and to give it a new future. No one need be ashamed, or need boast, of a liking, for instance, for Captain Marryat. To write a good story it was no longer held necessary to have the magniloquence of Scott, the learning of Charles Reade, the patient, Fosco-like adroitness of Wilkie Collins. There was, in fact, a disposition in 'literary circles' to welcome any good story; and when *King Solomon's Mines* came out, in 1885, it owed a great deal of its success to glory reflected from *Treasure Island*. In vain did stern and upright critics point

---

[1] *The Shakespeare Head Edition of the Novels and Selected Writings of Daniel Defoe.* Oxford: Blackwell. *The Duchy Edition of the Tales and Romances of Sir Arthur Quiller-Couch.* Dent. *The Works of Stanley J. Weyman.* Murray. *The Lively Peggy.* By Stanley J. Weyman. Murray.

out the difference. In vain did young William Archer declare that the style of the newer book 'is alternately flat and tawdry, always slipshod, and often incorrect', and that the author of it was 'merely a popular paper-stainer'. In vain did young Mr J. M. Robertson write of 'the essential vulgarity of plan, aim, and method'. The yarn was being backed by Andrew Lang, whose fear of being associated with the shop sometimes, perhaps, a little unsettled his judgement. And it was felt to be rather grand to say that style and so forth did not matter so long as the yarn was good. Let us remember that this was in the eighteen-eighties, and some people, at any rate, were talking a good deal about Henry James, and about Flaubert and the *mot juste*. And there was Stevenson himself, cracking sky-high the works of Alexandre Dumas the elder, which well brought up young men had been taught to regard as beneath contempt.

Perhaps there was no danger really. But looking back now, it seems as if the rattling good yarn might then have followed a Gadarene path if men of letters had not headed it back. In 1887 there was published a book entitled *Dead Man's Rock*. Rumour told Oxford undergraduates of the time (and in the author's new preface to the book there is nothing to contradict the rumour) that it was admiration for *Treasure Island* which had spurred Couch of Trinity to try his hand at a yarn, and that it was the success of his venture that led him to give up the academic for the literary career. Let not the lure of old memories persuade us to see the effect of *Dead Man's Rock* more than honourably magnified. But it was a rattling good yarn, and it was (as writers say) 'written'. Widely different though Stevenson and 'Q' very obviously are, *Dead Man's Rock* was able to join, in those days, *Treasure Island* as a good yarn by a man of letters; and the yarn, as a class, was saved from falling back into a contempt from which it had been too suddenly lifted. Two years later came *The Splendid Spur*. This story of a boy's adventures in the English Civil War was another good yarn. Read anew all these years later, it seems a little perfunctory, as if this 'cloak-and-sword stuff' did not come natural to the writer. But the date is interesting. In the following year, 1890, another new writer, Stanley J. Weyman, published another 'cloak-and-sword' yarn, *The House of the Wolf*. A tale about the massacre of St Bartholomew, it was a childish affair, even compared with *The Splendid Spur*. But it fitted in with the other influences at work. Stevenson, 'Q', Weyman—these three were enough to win for romance (as it used to be called) the place in the sun from which the advocates of 'realism' and the 'slice of life' wanted to oust it. And Weyman, being less versatile and more easily copied than 'Q', exercised more direct influence on younger writers. The early work of Mr A. E. W. Mason, for instance, cannot but have owed something to *The House of the Wolf* and *A Gentleman of France*. Indeed, while bookishness in some quarters was turning yellower and yellower, the libraries had a very large supply of cloak-and-sword yarns, dated in one of the more picturesque periods of history, in most of which the narrator was a rather tiresomely obtuse young man and the heroine as shrewish to him as ever was Linet to Sir Beaumains

The writers of these yarns (to digress for a moment) usually hampered themselves by letting the hero tell the story himself. Mr Percy Lubbock has very ably pointed out the advantages of this form of narration. One of its disadvantages will be plain from two quotations. The first is from *The House of the Wolf*. The hero, a mere boy, has just killed the ringleader of a mob:

> I set my foot upon his neck. 'Hounds! Beasts!' I cried, not loudly this time, for though I was like one possessed with rage, it was inward rage, 'go to your kennels!'

What self-consciousness in the turmoil! What a memory, nearly fifty years after the event! The other quotation is from *Dead Man's Rock*, from a page (21 of the new edition) which contains also a little puzzle about the relative positions and movements of the two characters. The narrator is a boy of eight, and this is what he writes about the strange man whom he saw on the sands:

The most curious feature about the man was the air of nervous expectation that marked, not only his face, but every movement of his body.

It is not as serious a lapse as the other, but again the voice of the author is heard with disillusioning clearness through the mask of the character. It would be very difficult, probably impossible, to catch Defoe out making such a mistake. Over and over again he demands acceptance of a convention. He will, for instance, make Moll write down a long conversation that she only heard by report. But he never makes slips that bring disillusion suddenly. To end this digression, it may be admitted that it is hardly fair on the two modern authors to take examples from the first story of each. But what if they both outgrew (as indeed they both did) such youthful errors, while many another romancer did not?

Romance—story-telling—a yarn—who thinks about defining these terms looks back upon a sea strewn with wrecks and forward to foaming reefs. Fortunately the authors before us can be discussed without going farther than what is commonly understood and accepted. In his *Aspects of the Novel* Mr E. M. Forster writes:

We are all like Scheherazade's husband, in that we want to know what happens next. That is universal and that is why the backbone of a novel has to be a story. Some of us want to know nothing else— there is nothing in us but primeval curiosity, and consequently our other literary judgements are ludicrous. And now the story can be defined. It is a narrative of events arranged in their time sequence— dinner coming after breakfast, Tuesday after Monday, decay after death, and so on. *Qua* story, it can only have one merit: that of making the audience want to know what happens next. And, conversely, it can only have one fault: that of making the audience not want to know what happens next. These are the only two criticisms that can be made on the story that is a story. It is the lowest and simplest of literary organisms. Yet it is the highest factor common to all the very complicated organisms known as novels.

In Nature, we believe, there is no such thing as H_2O: chemists have to make it. In literature there is certainly no such thing as Mr Forster's 'story that is a story'. True, to study the railway bookstalls and to read a 'best-seller' or two about crime and its detection is to wonder whether Mr Forster is not right—whether it is not indeed possible and even easy to abstract again and again, and very quickly, a pure story from what professes to be a narrative of things done by and words spoken by human beings. But it cannot be so. No writer can do for a tale what a chemist can do for water—so divest it of all that is natural, human, and common to experience that it is left a pure story. Why do we want to know what happens next? Partly because the story is about beings whom we are content for the moment to accept as human beings, in places which might conceivably exist on this earth, and in situations which do not defy the laws of Nature though they may strain the belt of probability. A pure story, in fact (could such a thing be made), would interest nobody. Mr Forster has been too coldly scientific, because the story is the element of a novel which interests him the least. And happily all the three story-tellers with whom we are now concerned have brows far too noble for his cap to fit. *Moll Flanders* is a story, a narrative of events arranged in their time sequence. And why do we want to know what happened to Moll Flanders? Mr Forster himself can tell us:

Moll is a character physically, with hard, plump limbs, that get into bed and pick pockets. She lays no stress upon her appearance, yet she moves us as having height and weight, as breathing and eating, and doing many of the things that are usually missed out.... Whatever she does gives us a slight shock—not the jolt of disillusionment, but the thrill that proceeds from a living being.

So with Singleton and Colonel Jack, and still more with Roxana, the 'fortunate mistress'. And so with Harry Revel and Simon Colliver and John à Cleeve and Jack Marvel; and so, in lower degree, with Anne, Vicomte de Caylus, and Colonel John Sullivan and the Captain of Vlaye. A story, at any rate, is not compelled to leave out all other claims to interest. It may partake, while it remains a story, of the qualities of what Mrs Wharton describes as novels of character and novels of situation. It may even go as deep into character

54

and thought as some of those more recent works of fiction, which are like the *Anti-Jacobin's* knife-grinder: 'Story! God bless you! I have none to tell, sir.' And one other common reproach against the story may be touched upon. The story that is a story is supposed to begin at an arbitrary point and to stop at an arbitrary point. It is merely a length chopped off. But it is common experience that life runs more or less in sections: this or that, as we say, begins a new chapter, or ends a chapter. And the story that is content to be episodical may be found to have a juster end than one that aims at a more imposing finality. It may be found to have a truer unity than a carefully constructed plot, because its unity is based on the truth of a single character.

Neither of the two moderns before us was content to remain a story-teller in the sense in which we have been using the word. (Nor, we would add, has another, Mr A. E. W. Mason, who, always an admirable craftsman, soon began to look for better stuff to work upon.) In his very first book, innocent, thrilling little yarn as it is of dark streets and torches and mobs, of terrors and escapes and sword-play and tushery and swash-buckling, Stanley Weyman had a little try at an odd piece of character. Taking a hint from De Thou, he accords to his mighty villain a revenge very different from what the reader has been expecting. And to follow Stanley Weyman's career is to see him, not very consistently but every now and then, trying hard to write a real novel, complete with plot (not episode) and character (not dummy). There is some character in *A Gentleman of France*; but the attempt at plot resulted in a notable anti-climax. There is good construction in *Chippinge*, but feeble character. Stanley Weyman is always most enjoyable when he is writing history. He was fond of history for its own sake, and did not merely cram it up in order to write yarns about it. The account of the Reform Bill in *Chippinge* deserves all the commendation for use in schools that Mr Alfred Tresidder Sheppard would probably give it: it is interesting even to adult readers who know something about the subject. But the adult reader cannot find himself more than tepidly interested in the hero and the heroine. That is not due to any carelessness in the telling of the story. Indeed, Weyman showed a fine artistic ingenuity in fitting together the political and the private pieces in the jig-saw. He showed his ingenuity too clearly. So far from throwing, in his occasional manner, episode after episode, he laboured at making a whole. He fitted it all so closely that the hero had to give way to the history. He had not the life-giving touch. He could make a fight live, indeed, but not a man nor a woman. Leave out the tushery and the history, and what remains will fall down. In the new book, *The Lively Peggy*, there is no history, and no fighting that we see. It is a story of the Devon coast in the Napoleonic War. *The Lively Peggy* is a privateer; she is also the rector's younger daughter, who runs away with a naval officer dismissed for being drunk on duty. The girl and the ship are very carefully woven together. The story-teller sees to it that the more prominent scenes shall be as moving as he can make them. There is no violation of probability in character or incident; and all that the author meant by the rector, his cold-blooded elder daughter, and a jolly girl who comes to the heroine's rescue is clearly brought out. The whole is a respectable piece of work which leaves the reader rather sad, because it has sterling qualities, yet lacks the imaginative insight into men and women, lacks the touch which gives life not to characters only but to setting and scenery, lacks above all the humour which is the very fire of creation. And so Stanley Weyman, good historian, careful craftsman, vigorous story-teller, never rose to be a good novelist.

For the other modern, it became clear forty years ago that 'Q' did not mean to remain a story-teller only. The book that followed *Dead Man's Rock* was *Troy Town* (and never be it forgotten that to readers in general *Troy Town* gave, through the two sea-going friends of Mr Caleb Trotter, the first taste of a sort of verse composed not only by Miss Plinlimmon but by Mr Quiller-Couch, and by Professor Sir Arthur as well). In literature, indeed (and literature has not exacted all his energy), 'Q' has all along been 'stretcht out to all things, and with all content'. But here our business is with his fiction only. And the first and chiefest thing to be said about his fiction is that, with all its faults, it is crowded with live people. The yellow-faced woman and her villainous son in *Dead Man's Rock* can at least hold their own against any similar pieces in the game of yarning; but there is no need to call on them. Take *Harry Revel*, which the new little foreword (there is a new preface to every volume) well calls 'a story which either explains itself or cannot be exculpated'—the most casual, loosely stitched, wilful, shirt-sleeve piece of yarning that even 'Q' ever did—and make the acquaintance of Miss Plinlimmon and Lydia Belcher and Benjamin Jope. Jump the great gulf that separates *Harry Revel* from *Hetty Wesley*, and watch reverence, sympathy and robust sense working together to show a great and beautiful nature in trouble. Thence another leap to *The Mayor of Troy*; to *True Tilda*; and then to where a pause is necessary, *The Westcotes*. It is a very far cry from *Dead Man's Rock* or *The Splendid Spur* to the story of dear Miss Dorothea Westcote, who trusted and was deceived. And still we have not glanced at *The Ship of Stars*, a complete and four-square novel, nor at *Foe-Farrell*, that sudden and convincing excursion into a subtly analytic kind of fiction that even 'Q' had not tried before.

It is all rather bewildering. And yet it is all unmistakably the work of one mind, though in many moods. The method is always that of the story-teller: 'the plain objective style, old as Boccaccio, far older', as he calls it; the method that begins at the beginning, goes on till it comes to the end and then— stops? Well, not with 'Q' always. It cannot be denied that, like Fletcher, he sometimes 'huddles up' his ends. He has got what he wanted out of the tale; so now to have done with it! It is part of the story-teller in 'Q' to get rather quickly tired of his story. There are so many stories to tell, and so many things to do. His mind is masterful, not laborious. Some of his keenest admirers have been waiting, waiting for the great novel which we were convinced he had it in him to write. We have got *The Ship of Stars*, which is one of the best novels of the time. And we have got *The Westcotes*, which one might dare to call perfect on its small and dainty scale. We have got *Hetty Wesley*, and love it none the less because the classifiers will always be bothered about which pigeon-hole to put it in. We have got some of the best short stories in the English language. And still we are not quite satisfied. Perhaps a smaller output—a closer labour—

Nevertheless, to this story-teller, who has never for a moment lost the true story-teller's enjoyment of his story, we owe something more than all the fun and excitement and sorrow he has given us. Like many an English writer, he has ideas of virtue at heart, to colour, not to deflect his stories. He believes that thought and conduct matter; and can warm his stories with his ideal, yet never (as does another living story-teller) fret his reader's nerves. He delights in any kind of oddity, Cornish or other, from the religion of Squire Moyle to the shyness of Mr Fogo; and to his love of symmetry and beauty we owe Taffy Raymond no less than the pick of those descriptions (take as a fair example the Canadian forest in the fifth chapter of *Fort Amity*) which show equally well his power of writing prose and his power of making scenes and persons live. Behind all his vigour and all his none too carefully managed skill lies a quality of mind which is best called winning. His faithful readers more than admire his books; they love them.

STEVENSON AFTER FIFTY YEARS

(1938)

Sitting by the grave of the poor Franciscan monk, pulling out the little horn-box that once had been his, and plucking up a nettle or two which had no business to grow there, Laurence Sterne burst into a flood of tears. But, he pleads, 'I am as weak as a woman; and I beg the world not to smile, but pity me.' Psha! Mountebank! Sniveller! Posture-maker! Coward! With your blubber and your cheap dribble, you brought upon your head the manly contempt of a Thackeray, and you have never recovered from it. Why could you not be more like Dean Swift, who 'laughed his hearty great laugh out of his broad chest as nature bade him', as manly and robust as any Porthos or Friar Tuck? Or—not having a broad chest, but only a lean and consumptive one to laugh out of, you might at least have written something like this: 'No more land of counterpane for me. To be drowned, to be shot, to be thrown from a horse—aye, to be hanged, rather than pass again through that slow dissolution.' Thackeray would have thought that manly to heroism; the Edwardians and late Victorians did think it so. It was left for the neo-Georgians, cold-eyed, disillusioned realists, to find in Swift's 'hearty great laugh' the jesting of a soul in agony, in Sterne's tears the defiant parade of a known weakness, in Stevenson's talk of shooting and hanging a childish reaction against mere illness, and in each of the three a sick man (Swift in mind, the other two in body) keeping his end up as bravely as he knew how.

Both Sterne and Stevenson (like Oscar Wilde in *De Profundis*) were heartening themselves by what in children is called showing-off. Stevenson's attitude was obviously the most vulnerable, because it was the most likely to be taken as the true measure. But Stevenson had bad luck. Andrew Lang, so easily bored with anything earnest and, as we should now say, high-brow, welcomed this gallant playboy from his own country who could sweat for the *mot juste* with the best of the Bodley Head men, to use it in a yarn or a farce. The authorized biography by Graham Balfour put the halo on the hero-saint. And then Henley, who happened to know something himself about pain and counterpane and loved the blunt truth even better than he loved Stevenson, shied a stone at the painted glass and cracked it. Even ardent Stevensonians took fright. One of them (we quote from a privately printed lecture of 1901) declared that

Stevenson has suffered far more from indiscriminate praise than from adverse criticism. His attractive personality and affectionate nature turned a wide circle of his contemporaries into a sort of Society for the Propagation of R. L. Stevenson's fame.

And then, most unkindest cut of all, came the Great War. Stevenson, the heroic sufferer, was clean wiped out by a few odd millions of inarticulate lumps of tortured flesh and blood; Stevenson, the apostle of action, was a crier of fish that stank in every nostril; Stevenson, the unconquerably cheerful in adversity, dwindled to a pretentious and puerile babbler. His reputation as man and as writer was never so low as it was (*teste* this *Supplement* at the time) in the early post-War years.

None of this was Stevenson's fault; it was his bad luck, and it should turn to his good fortune. There is no need to lament the roughness which scraped off the spurious paint, so long as it left the genuine unharmed. What would be lamentable would be that the modern age should go on being deterred by Stevenson's late Victorian innocence from seeing him fairly. These last twenty years have done something. In December, 1919, a writer in this *Supplement* suggested that his physical inadequacy had endowed 'with the audacity of literature one who would, under other conditions, have forsworn the audacious in life'. The refutation of that idea can be found in the very same number of the *Supplement*, in a long letter written by Mr W. R. Lysaght to describe a week's visit to Stevenson, to Tusitala, in effect the ruler of Samoa, while the woods were full of a rebellious chieftain's warriors. The writer of an article on Stevenson in this *Supplement* last July made no bones about claiming for him a crowded adventurous life as traveller, as lover, 'literally taking his life in his hand to rejoin his beloved across seas and mountains', and as feudal chieftain in Samoa; and he did not fail to go forward to the true matter—that these audacious adventures were 'neither irrelevant accidents to his writing, nor clogs on his self-expression'.

The immediate post-War England could not accept the heroic Stevenson; it must see him as a rather silly boy, showing off. The English reader of to-day dare not dictate views of Stevenson to Stevenson's own countrymen; but he is not likely to recognize a Stevenson who has somehow got mixed up with Byron—with the Gordon in Byron—and who must shout down his own sense of sin. We must believe that what seems brave, sunny, happy in Stevenson was not mere mouthing and prancing but a genuine quality which he hoped the world would observe—for its own good. We must accept him as entirely sincere, because only so can we find the true level between his feverish ups and downs. Reaction against his lifelong illness and reaction against his early religious training must be allowed to this extent—that he liked not to falsify but to stop short of his vision of truth. It is commonly supposed, perhaps, that he did this by lingering in the playgrounds of boyhood. Some of that looking backward was wilful; and those who indulge in it inevitably pay for it with some of their manhood. In Stevenson there was some genuine childishness, such as his love of dressing-up, recorded by Mr Lysaght. There was also some genuine, unaffected boyishness in him. It is at least permissible to suggest, though not to insist, that his left-handedness in love-stories was due to fear of Victorian prudery than to the nice reticence of a growing boy, whose core of modesty is untainted, no matter what bawdry he may talk among his fellows. How much of his moralizing is more than the anxiety of the big brother that the little brother shall not do the family disgrace?

Of this boyishness, organic or protective, it is possible to make too much. Stevenson grew to manhood; and the lack in him is a lack found in many, in most, grown men. It is a lack of thought. But not many grown men can claim, as Stevenson could claim, that their shrinking up from thought is due not to idleness, nor to fear, but to pure fastidiousness of taste. In the letter from Mr Lysaght there is one illuminating passage. He told Stevenson what Meredith had said—that 'his banishment from the great world of men, his inability to keep in close touch with the social development of the time, might be a disadvantage to his work'. Stevenson protested that if a man wanted his work to be good and not merely popular, it was all the better for him 'to be removed from these London influences. Human nature is always the same, and you see and understand it better when you are standing outside the crowd.' His mention of popularity and of London influences shows how far he was from facing Meredith's objection and from admitting even to himself that 'the social development of the time' was not at all what he wanted to keep in touch with. His head was so full of a number of things that it had no room for that. His fellow-countryman, young Mr Barrie, was soon to show in *Sentimental Tommy* and in *Tommy and Grizel* that he had looked at manly pretence more bravely and thoughtfully than Stevenson had ever dared to; and by the time of *The Admirable Crichton* he was already, compared with Stevenson, a profound thinker. There is no need to call in Meredith, Hardy, Herman Melville, nor even a brother poet, romancer and essayist, 'Q', all of whom could knock Stevenson into a cocked hat as a thinker. To blame a man for not doing what he never meant to do is a vice which criticism shows small sign of outgrowing; and if, with our critic of 1919, we say of Stevenson: 'Wise he was, but in that common sense that religion may welcome but Art must refuse', we had better be careful that Meredith is not listening.

It was the artist in Stevenson that knew what was and what was not his country and with scarcely an exception declined to trespass. Those who are quite sure that they have outgrown the wisdom of *Virginibus Puerisque* must be very poor readers if they cannot still read those four essays with pleasure, not in the technicalities of English prose, but in the manner in which this very delightful person expresses his sensible notions— aware that he is thought delightful and his manner charming, but well able to carry it off. To read *Virginibus* is, for a mature reader, to put Stevenson to the sharpest trial possible; *The Lantern Bearers* and *Old Mortality*, on the other hand, has each its own perfection, its impermeable unity. We may lay down *Yvette*, or *Un Cœur Simple* and sigh that Stevenson never wrote stories like that. He never tried to; and, if it comes to telling stories, would not the story, in his *Edinburgh*, about the two old sisters who shared a room and quarrelled over theology suffice to make a man's reputation, without *Markheim*, or *The Sire de Malétroit's Door*?

In the long stories we are on shakier ground—even if we contrive to leave Scott out of it for once. It is here that the smallness of Stevenson's very pretty wineglasses of thought and feeling becomes most apparent; and even Mr A. E. W. Mason, who knows what it is to labour at making a novel, finds that 'the reader is at times more aware of the craftsmanship and of the exquisite selection of a word than of the story'. That is true, even of *Treasure Island* and of *Catriona*; all the same, there is Pew and there is Alan Breck; and there is the fragment of *Weir of Hermiston* to show, as some think, what maturity would have brought. A generation that dares to enjoy its pot of honey without sitting on a grave or grumbling that it is not caviare will surely find something to its account in the grace and gaiety which this picksome artist wrought out of a good deal of mental and physical suffering. He was no humbug, though he liked you to see how clever he was; and his peculiar quality lasts on.

ADVENTURES OF A NOVEL

(1941)

Fifty years ago yesterday, on 4 July 1891, the *Graphic* published the first instalment of a new novel by Thomas Hardy entitled *Tess of the D'Urbervilles*. Hardy had settled down to the writing of the story in the autumn of 1889. Three editors had asked him for the serial rights in his next novel. *Murray's Magazine* had asked first, and to *Murray's*, in October 1890, he submitted as much of it as he had written. In November it was returned to him, declined 'virtually on the score of its improper explicitness'. *Macmillan's Magazine* had been second on the list; and *Macmillan's* lost no time in doing what *Murray's* had done and on the same grounds. Thereupon Hardy, who wanted the money for the serial rights, tried a new plan. He cut out certain portions which he thought might be the causes of offence. He modified others, taking care to write the modified versions in different coloured ink so as to find them again easily when the time should come. Having made these changes with 'cynical amusement', he sent the story in its revised form to the *Graphic*, and the *Graphic* accepted it.

Publication once begun, the editor stuck to it. But he declined to print the scene in Chapter XIV of the christening of the dying infant Sorrow by his girl-mother with her sleepy little brothers and sisters kneeling round; and he funked the scene in Chapter XXIII in which Angel Clare carries the four milkmaids, one after another, across the pool. Hardy—doubtless with more 'cynical amusement'—substituted a wheelbarrow for Angel's arms. The christening he sent to the *Fortnightly Review*, which printed it in May 1891, as 'The Midnight Baptism, a Study in Christianity'. Another episode to which he had from the first decided not to subject the readers of the *Graphic* was the 'jig' at the market and fair of Chaseborough (Chapter x) which led to the seduction. That went to Henley, who printed it in a special literary supplement to the *National Observer* on 14 November 1891, under the title of 'Saturday Night in Arcady'. This was the new plan— to place where they would be valued such portions of a story as the general run would reject. Hardy did not try it when the time came for him to tone down *Jude the Obscure* for *Harper's Magazine*; and after that, as we know, he had no need of it. But for *Tess* it worked satisfactorily.

The toning-down of *Tess*, as we have seen, involved more than the gain of the wheelbarrow and the loss of the christening and the dance. For certain reasons too well known to students, research among books and periodicals is not just at present as easy as usual in this country; and it is a stroke of happiest fortune that brings to hand at such a moment such a book as Mr Carl J. Weber's *Hardy of Wessex*, which was briefly noticed in this *Supplement* on 31 May last. Mr Weber, an erudite authority on Hardy, is especially strong on *Tess*, a novel which he has edited in a volume that ought not to be at the service only of his fellow-Americans. In *Hardy of Wessex* he gives a laughable, lamentable and doubtless trustworthy account of what Hardy did to *Tess* in order to make it palatable to readers of the *Graphic* in 1891. The seduction (it would surely be better if all were agreed to call it by its true name, the rape) of Tess was turned into a mock marriage. Tess had consented to be married to Alec secretly and by special licence, as she told her mother:

to get rid of his pestering. I drove with him to Melchester, and there in a private room I went through the form of marriage with him as before a registrar. A few weeks after, I found out that it was not the registrar's house we had gone to, as I had supposed, but the house of a friend of his, who had played the part of the registrar. I then came away from Trantridge instantly, though he wished me to stay; and here I am.

That change meant that the story told by Tess to Angel Clare on their wedding night at Wellbridge must be changed too. Hardy was pretty rough-handed over that:

> She entered on her story of the visit with D'Urberville to the supposed Registrar's, her abiding sense of the moral validity of the contract, and her wicked flying in the face of that conviction by wedding again.

But he spared no pains nor courage to square the doings at Sandridge with the new version. It would never do to let Tess and Alec be living together in the lodgings as Mr and Mrs D'Urberville. 'Miss D'Urberville' lodges there alone. 'Part of the first floor had been taken for her by a cousin who sometimes occupied another apartment.' Living alone, as Mr Weber demurely explains, 'Miss D'Urberville sometimes was made to soliloquize about her cousin, whom she was shortly called upon to murder. And this is not a hack dramatist adapting a French farce for the English stage; it is Thomas Hardy adapting his own *Tess of the D'Urbervilles*. One more little rub is perhaps worth mentioning. A 'gentleman with daughters', wrote to say that the bloodstain on the ceiling in the landlady's room—that ghastly 'scarlet blot' that 'had the appearance of a gigantic ace of hearts'—was 'indecent'. So, no doubt, was the eyeless face of Oedipus or the 'poor, poor dumb mouths' in the dead body of Caesar. But—the indecency having got into the *Graphic*—Hardy was saved the trouble of cutting it out and then putting it back when he prepared his story for publication in book form.

It is not surprising that he found that restoration heavy collar-work. It must be admitted that he showed more detachment than most genuine artists can show concerning the integrity of their offspring. Persuading himself that he wrote novels mainly for a living, he could play the indifferent with an air. When he sold the film rights, he declined to make a single suggestion or take the slightest interest; and he heard with complete composure that the film people had given the story a 'happy' ending. There may have been—there must have been—a touch of affectation about the outward serenity; but we are entitled to believe most firmly in an inward serenity which was the lonely confidence of the creator who has made a new thing and seen that it was good. He had written *Tess of the D'Urbervilles*; and for the first time had written what he himself thought and felt, with no regard to public opinion or taste. *Tess of the D'Urbervilles* had being—not, of course, the ideal being of the novel that he had imagined and, but for human limitations, would have written, but nearer to that ideal state than any of his novels had been before; at any rate absolute and complete in itself; a being that could take no harm from the partial and relative existence of something that pretended to be *Tess of the D'Urbervilles* and was not. To prepare that simulacrum had been a bitter joke at the public expense; to get the real thing down again on paper was a bore. But *Tess* was still *Tess*, and he the maker of it.

The book was published in November 1891 by Osgood, McIlvaine and Co. in three volumes. By July of the following year a fifth edition, in one volume, was called for. Without getting tangled up in distinctions between 'greatest', 'best', 'most powerful', 'artistically most perfect', and so forth, we may say that there was that in *Tess* which first raised Hardy to his throne among the classics. The public was led captive. It scolded, it sneered, it sniggered; but it surrendered, as it had had never surrendered to Hardy before and was not to surrender to *Jude the Obscure*, always the favourite of the adventurous few. This present article is concerned rather with the history of the novel than with its quality; and its history consists in great measure of savage attack. But that attack is never directed against it as a novel but as an expression of social opinion and a view of personal morality. The fuss could not have been half so noisy if the story had not seemed to its readers so 'real'. Here and there, as all its lovers know, the machinery of *Tess* creaks; but the mishap is soon overwhelmed by the abundant reality of the whole. Is there any other novel so richly English? Nine centuries of England link the Norman D'Urbervilles with the peasant girl in whom their lineaments were still traceable and their blood still potent. In the Chase at Trantridge, with its primeval oaks and yews, a sinister neighbour for the smug prosperity of the sham D'Urbervilles; in the lush dairy-farm in the Vale, and the starve-acre uplands of Flintcomb-Ash, there is an inexhaustible abundance of the fundamental life of England. Whenever that life touches in the story a life less close in Nature, it asserts itself almost violently. Tess in her smart dressing-gown facing Angel Clare in the early morning in the lodgings at Sandridge wrenches the mind most painfully back to Tess in her bed-gown running up the ladder before dawn to wake Angel Clare for the early milking. And when Angel's clergyman brothers and Miss Mercy Chant find in the hedge the thick boots which Tess had carefully hidden there against her long walk home, and carry them off 'for some poor person', sure that they must have belonged to a tramp, or to some impostor who wanted to excite sympathy by going barefoot into the town, the three of them are known for poor, false, flickering wraiths against the abundant and abiding reality of the English life in which and out of which Tess had grown to be what she was.

Much of the outcry was caused by the ignorance of urban and 'cultured' readers who did not know that such a life existed, nor imagined that, ancient and powerful as it was, it would have conventions, rules and tendencies of its own, not all to be fitted into the convention of politer social grades. This ignorance and lack of imagination misled readers of much higher intelligence than the common run, to whom Tess was 'a little harlot' who 'deserved hanging'. Stevenson wrote to Barrie about someone's mistress: 'She was what Hardy calls (and others in their plain way don't) a Pure Woman'; and it must have been a similar sneer from Stevenson which caused the difference between Henry James's opinion of 'the good little Thomas Hardy's' book in March 1892—'chock-full of faults and falsity and yet has a singular beauty and charm', and Henry James's opinion of the same book in February 1893:

Oh yes, dear Louis, she is vile. The pretence of 'sexuality' is only equalled by the absence of it, and the abomination of the language by the author's reputation for style. There are indeed some pretty smells and sights and sounds.

One contemporary stated his objections with good sense and dignity. But even Lionel Johnson went astray. He began with a just and pertinent condemnation of the occasional general reflections on Nature, convention and so forth as faults in literary art, not in ethics or biology or metaphysics. He wandered from that secure ground into a very shaky position on what he very strangely did not see to be the opposite side. He complained that these occasional general reflections did not make a consistent philosophy. Every word of what he says in condemnation of the consistent philosophy which he does not find in those occasional reflections is a reply to his strictures on the faulty art that introduced them. The more spontaneously they came to the author's pen on the spur of the very moment in the story, the less likely they were to fit together in a consistent scheme.

It may be possible to fashion out of this particular novel (the author meanwhile protesting loudly against such a liberty with his story) a philosophy which is easily bowled over. Such a triumph in skittles can have not the slightest damaging effect upon the sumptuous yet awful beauty, the heartrending but heart-softening sadness of the story of that particular girl. But the very difficulty in defining that philosophy goes to prove that the incidental general reflections grew out of the story and were emotional rather than intellectual in origin. And in the queer history of this book there are two striking instances of sudden impulse. Each gave an obvious cause of offence to readers who might not otherwise have noticed that there was anything in the story to be offended at. Hardy had restored the mutilated work to its complete form. Says Mr Weber:

> At the very last minute, after reading the final proofs, Hardy had another afterthought. His original title, 'A Daughter of the D'Urbervilles', had given way to the more familiar phrasing. He now added the words: 'A Pure Woman, Faithfully Presented by Thomas Hardy.'

In all innocence, he believed that to be 'an estimate that nobody would be likely to dispute'. To-day, when we have all read our Havelock Ellis, it is difficult to imagine how outrageously disputable such an estimate seemed fifty years ago—even though we remember that the nineties made rather a pet of Sin, especially the sins of the flesh. Whatever his private opinion, no man nowadays may doubt that others honestly find unsullied purity—what Lascelles Abercrombie called Tess's 'intense spiritual chastity'—in a girl who had lost her virginity through force and later abandoned her body to her seducer only when, to her thinking, it had ceased to have any spiritual existence because her husband had no love for it and for her. There is one weak spot in Hardy's claim; and it is surprising that not more has been made of it. It comes near the end of Chapter XII, and hints lightly but plainly at what happened at Trantridge between the night of the fair and Tess's return home.

The other impulse caused an equal or greater outcry upon a far more superficial matter. In the manuscript sent to *The Graphic*, says Mr Weber, the last paragraph of the book began:

'"Justice" was done. The two speechless gazers bent themselves down to the earth.' Between those two sentences he now inserted the words: 'and Time, the Arch-satirist, had had his joke out with Tess.'

Nearly twenty years were to pass before Hardy took *Time's Laughing-Stocks* for the title of a book; but his readers must already have been familiar with the idea, or the fancy; and no one, probably, would have objected to the notion of Time as the 'Arch-satirist'. The phrase is too vague and decorative to get excited about. It was otherwise with the second impulse over the same passage. When he prepared the story for publication as a book, he once more wrote out:

'Justice' was done. The two speechless gazers bent themselves down to the earth, as if in prayer, and remained thus a long time, absolutely motionless: the flag continued to wave [corrected from 'waving'] silently.

And then (it may all be followed in the facsimile in *The Early Life of Thomas Hardy*) he had another afterthought. After 'done' he interlined:

& the President of the Immortals (in Æschylean phrase) had ended his sport with Tess. And the D'Urberville knights & dames slept on in their tombs unknowing.

It was an impulse that he had better have resisted. The brackets that he put round 'in Æschylean phrase' show much more clearly than the now usual commas that the words were intended to apply only to 'the President of the Immortals', which is merely Buckley's (1849) rendering of two words in the *Prometheus Bound* which the Loeb translation gives as 'Prince of the Blessed'. No one would have pretended to think that Hardy really believed Time to get any fun out of torturing Tess. It was different when he transferred the fancy to the (or to a) Supreme Being. Critics found in it cause to accuse Hardy of misunderstanding or misrepresenting Aeschylus. Doubtless, he wanted to link his tragedy with the great Greek tragedies; and doubtless he forgot for the moment that a complete Greek tragedy had three parts, of which the last told of reconciliation and hope. Walter Lock was right when he said that *Tess* was 'the *Agamemnon* without the other two'. But Hardy's little indiscretion did not deserve the belabouring it received—a trouncing which very likely sharpened (for use ere long in *Jude the Obscure*) his suspicion of the attitude of men who have learned Greek at school or college to men who have picked up Greek for themselves. Unfortunately, moreover, his self-defence was maladroit— was, even, a little disingenuous. His President of the Immortals could not but seem something more than 'the forces opposed to Tess allegorized as a personality'; and 'Aeolus maliciously tugged at her garments and tore her hair in his wrath' ought not to be seriously advanced as an equivalent personification. And even supposing that:

> As flies to wanton boys are we to the gods,
> They kill us for their sport

71

were words written by William Shakespeare as his own opinion and not spoken by the Earl of Gloucester, a character in a play, they could be countered with the remark that the same writer ascribes to Gloucester's son:

> The gods are just, and of our pleasant vices
> Make instruments to plague us.

The gods that killed Tess killed also Alec Stoke, called D'Urberville.

WHAT HAPPENS IN 'HAMLET'[1]

(1935)

No one, said Walkley, not even Shakespeare, has ever seen Shakespeare's Hamlet on the stage. On the grounds of the theatre's inability to express the author's conception he was defending the theatre's right to present what conception should at any time best please itself. In effect, his was the same attitude as that of the cinema man in America who pleaded for *The Taming of the Shrew* because: 'Yes—it is Shakespeare—but we're turning it into comedy.'

Walkley chose Hamlet for his illustration probably because all through his own experience of the theatre he had been seeing actors turning Hamlet, the character, and with it *Hamlet*, the play, into something or other. It was not always so. Peering, like Miranda, into the dark backward, historians of the theatre report that *Hamlet* was more respected than any other of Shakespeare's plays by the reformers of the seventeenth and eighteenth centuries. Up till Garrick's later years (and even Garrick's reformation of *Hamlet*, recently discovered in the Folger Library, turns out to be less root-and-branch than contemporary accounts suggested) *Hamlet* was not among the plays which had to be chopped and crushed into shape because they had, in the eyes of that age, no shape of their own. There were varieties in the details, the 'business', of performance; and, as with every part, each player liked to do something which no other player had done; but in general *Hamlet* was a good straightforward, bustling, emotional play of action, which only needed trimming because of its exceptional length. Not until the nineteenth century, probably, was every actor expected to show a new 'reading' of Hamlet, which should

---

[1] *What Happens in 'Hamlet'.* By J. Dover Wilson. Cambridge University Press.

differ, not in detail but in fundamentals, from all the others. And then the impulse came not from the theatre but from the study. Andrew Bradley ('Quiet consummation have, And renowned be thy grave!') suggested that Henry Mackenzie may have been the first to see that Hamlet was not, as Johnson thought, 'rather an instrument than an agent'; and he went on to observe:

> How significant the fact (if it be the fact) that it was only when the slowly rising sun of Romance began to flush the sky that the wonder, beauty and pathos of this most marvellous of Shakespeare's creations began to be visible!

When Bradley wrote marvellous he probably meant marvellous: he meant that Hamlet was more wonderful, less ordinary, more mysterious than any other of Shakespeare's creations; and that word mysterious cuts the cable. When it became clear that Hamlet was less easily labelled and pigeon-holed than any other of Shakespeare's tragic characters, men spent more and more time and trouble in the very interesting but futile occupation of studying the play with no reference to the theatre, and the character with too little reference to the play. Then grew the critical vice of thinking of Hamlet as a 'real' man, not even as a character in a book, still less in a play—a vice from which even Bradley, who was one of the first to expose it, could not shake himself free (he can write that Hamlet's 'adoption of the pretence of madness may well have been due in part to fear of the reality', which is not even the same as saying that the play leaves it doubtful). And then grew also the corresponding critical vice of trying to interpret Hamlet through systems and philosophies and beliefs which could not have been known to Shakespeare, without taking any trouble to find out by what systems, philosophies, and beliefs the character could have been seen by Shakespeare and interpreted by his first audiences. And the more was written, the less like anything human did Hamlet come to appear.

Into this fog burst some rude flashes of common sense. 'Historical' criticism, with J. M. Robertson at its head, begged to remind the world that *Hamlet* was a stage-play: that its plot was an old and well-known story: that other people had written plays on it before: and that when Shakespeare wrote his version there were certain types of character, incidents and other theatrical items in fashion, which he, as a professional play-maker, would be sure to respect. Therefore, if there were any difficulties in *Hamlet*, they were to be explained simply enough by Shakespeare's failure, either through incompetence or through carelessness, to make his new play fit the old frame of the story. Constant readers of this *Supplement* may remember how this view of *Hamlet* roused wrath in Arthur Clutton-Brock and led to one of the best of the existing interpretations of *Hamlet* on the nineteenth-century lines. But much of modern criticism was content to see *Hamlet* as a muddle. It is admitted that in some plays (*Measure for Measure* is a favourite example) Shakespeare crammed his ideas maladroitly into the provided mould. So it must have been with *Hamlet*. But only one critic, so far as we know, had the wit to see and the courage to declare the due conclusion of criticism which should see in this undigested meal of a Cyclops the wine of psychology mingled with the gobbets of the old story. It was Mr T. S. Eliot who (first in the columns of this *Supplement*) made his much debated statement about *Hamlet*, that 'So far from being Shakespeare's masterpiece, the play is most certainly an artistic failure', and argued that

Hamlet's bafflement at the absence of objective equivalent to his feelings is a prolongation of the bafflement of his creator in the face of his artistic problem.

Such was the state of things when enter Professor Dover Wilson with his new book. There will be (it will be a thousand pities if there is not) some fine fighting over it; and the 'Epistle Dedicatory' to Dr W. W. Greg reveals that the author and Mr Granville-Barker have already been at it, hammer and tongs, before the book was published. But not the sharpest disagreement with what Dr Dover Wilson says could dull the reader to the delights of the way he says it. He has been twitted before now with his imagination and his enthusiasm; but imagination is no bad quality in the interpreter of high tragedy, especially when its eye is so firmly held to the object as in this book; and the enthusiasm, besides dissipating mists of convention and credulity, makes reading the book like sailing before the wind in the sunshine. But this final word of nearly twenty years' study of *Hamlet* is no mere entertainment. It is meant to reconstruct the meaning and force of the play, line by line, almost word by word, so that it may be understood as it has never been understood since it was new; the author's conviction being that *Hamlet* has been misjudged chiefly because no one has taken the trouble to work hard enough at understanding it.

In his edition of *Hamlet* for the New Shakespeare, published last year, Dr Dover Wilson wrote that in the study of a play

the establishment of the text comes first, then the interpretation of the dialogue, then the elucidation of the plot, and only after all these matters have been settled are we in a position to estimate character. ...Textual history, so far from being an instrument of dramatic criticism, as many modern Shakespearian students seem to imagine, is posterior not only to the three introductory stages just indicated, but also to that final appraisement of the play as a whole up to which they lead.

The text he examined and established in the two volumes added last year to the 'Shakespeare Problems' series; and he printed it in his edition of the play, where the interpretation of the dialogue was undertaken. The main purpose of the new book is to elucidate the plot by means of the interpretation of the dialogue in the 'established' text. Of the matter commonly called 'historical' criticism we have been warned to expect none. But Dr Dover Wilson is far from rejecting history and confining himself to an 'appreciation' from the standpoint of the twentieth-century mind. He is at one with Mr Eliot in this at least, that he sees the need of combining history and psychology. The difference lies in the kind of history employed. We begin with the fact that *Hamlet* was a stage play, not a history. Not a little has been written ere now about 'the requirements of the drama', and Shakespeare has by some been found guilty of reprehensible recklessness in twisting and maiming incident and character in order to keep his audience amused and conceal the defects of the story which he had chosen, or had been told, to rewrite. It has even been suggested that there is no hesitation in *Hamlet*, but that since the well-known plot had to be spun out to the regular length, Hamlet was made to imagine the delay and to accuse himself of it in soliloquy. No odder way could be found of hiding a trick to fill up time than making the hero himself call attention to it. Dr Dover Wilson's belief is that Shakespeare was not reckless nor clumsy, but that, having to fill his dramatic mould, he filled it not roughly, hoping that his audience would not notice, but with such masterly inventiveness and skill that the whole thing should be entirely explicable on examination, and should be also a firm and complete dramatic structure decorated with extraordinary subtlety and beauty.

Hamlet, again, is a stage play. That the story of the play is not known beforehand to the characters in it is not a new discovery. 'One must remember', wrote Bradley of Ophelia, 'that she had never read the tragedy'; but the new book insists also that the first audiences could not have known the story, if at all, anything like so well as we, who have more than a century of intensive study of it to affect our judgement. The aim must be, therefore, to put ourselves in the position, so far as it may be possible, of the original hearers, and to take this work of dramatic art step by step, as it moves forward, knowing nothing more than the original hearers knew. But that involves knowing as much as possible of what the original hearers knew, and so we come back to history as Dr Dover Wilson uses it.

Did Hamlet believe the Ghost? It is plain to all that a part of him, at any rate, leaped to conviction of the truth of what his 'prophetic soul' had more or less suspected. Yet when, having heard the Ghost's story, he cried, 'And shall I couple hell?' what precisely did he mean?—it is a principle of our

author that no word of dialogue shall be let go until it has
given up its last secret. The answer is that Hamlet, a Pro-
testant prince (for reasons which Dr Dover Wilson makes
plain), would be expected by his audience to hold certain
opinions about ghosts; and that in the 'cellarage scene' his
wild and whirling words, 'truepenny', 'pioner', 'mole', and so
on, would have left the audience in no doubt that he did hold
those opinions, at least enough to make him—from the very
first and not weeks afterwards when the impulse had worn
thin—subject to the belief that the Ghost might indeed be a
devil, abusing him to damn him. The little piece of the history
of thought clears the way at once for the Play-scene, when
that doubt was finally to be removed. So much else is to
happen between the first apparition and the Play-scene that
Hamlet's doubt cannot be the only cause of his inaction; but
it was a genuine doubt. Genuine also was his reluctance to
kill the King at prayer; and, again, it was not the cause of
his inaction. But what would be thought of a play in which
the hero sheltered himself behind pretexts which any child
could see he did not believe? History, again, as our author
uses it, that is to say, the way in which the audience at Globe
or Blackfriars would see things, insists that Claudius was in
Hamlet's eyes a usurper; and declares that his mother's incest
and adultery and the murder of his father would be quite
enough to prevent Hamlet's emotion from being 'in excess of
the facts as they appear'.

The settling of these few preliminary and elementary
points cannot fail to affect the understanding of the play as a
whole. We go forward to find that in Dr Dover Wilson's
hands all the play between the apparition and the end of the
Play-scene is full of dramatic interest, chiefly because he has
paid more attention than most to Claudius. We see an acute,
and a not unamusing, battle of wits, with Claudius nervously
trying to find out what Hamlet is up to and Hamlet gaining
time by misleading his uncle. The scene between Polonius
and Reynaldo is there to show the most observant that some
time has gone by, without calling more attention to it than it

78

would receive from the ordinary member of the audience. The outstanding novelty in this part of the work comes in the relations of Hamlet and Ophelia. Not a little of it is due, again, to an intensive and historical consideration of words and phrases—'fishmonger', 'nunnery', 'loose my daughter to him'. And the situation thus revealed seems to him to demand the alteration in the text which he introduced into his edition of the play—a very slight shifting of a stage direction in Act II, scene 2—so that the audience shall know for certain that Hamlet has overheard Polonius's plot to 'loose' Ophelia to him.

It is Dr Dover Wilson's own persuasiveness which may embolden some to ask whether, with the dialogue interpreted as he interprets it, the emendation is now necessary. Ophelia is Polonius's daughter, Laertes's sister. Hamlet has heard the King crooning over Laertes; and he knows Polonius for a devoted servant of the usurper. The family is suspect. Ophelia has not only repelled his letters and denied his access, she has also failed him when, in genuine misery, he came to her for sympathy. Now he has been 'sent for'; and, when he comes to himself out of deep brooding, he sees the girl, and finds her obviously waiting for him, since she has brought his gifts to return to him. His first words are ironical; his next distantly polite; his third remark, 'No, no, I never gave you aught', interpreted by Dr Dover Wilson as meaning that the woman he did give the presents to is dead, might also, perhaps, be seen as a harassed man's attempt to protect himself against a 'scene', tantamount, in fact, to 'For goodness' sake, go away and don't bother me.' Then he wakes up, and on her transparent excuse that it is he who has been unkind, he sees the trap. Convinced though we may be that Dr Dover Wilson's reading of this scene is correct, and that Hamlet, savage, brutal from start to finish, with no touch of tenderness in him, is talking not only to Ophelia but also at Claudius and Polonius, we may still ask whether he would not have known very well that they were in hiding without his having overheard the plot and without, it is needless to say, the clumsy inadvertent appearance of Polonius which the stage sometimes presents.

What Happens in 'Hamlet'

Dr Dover Wilson's account of the Play-scene, however, is that which already has aroused, and indubitably will arouse again, the sharpest discussion. It was Dr Greg's 'devilish ingenious, but damnably wrong' interpretation of this scene which nearly twenty years ago set our author off on his study of *Hamlet*. The Dumb Show was the difficulty. To the 'historical' critics, the Dumb Show has always been a godsend— so obviously to them an undigested gobbet of the old play. Dr Dover Wilson, correcting the common error that Dumb Shows had fallen out of use when Shakespeare's *Hamlet* was young (a correction which is more than borne out by an article on Dumb Shows in the current number of the *Review of English Studies*), argues that Shakespeare could not have done without it, and that, properly seen, it is one of the most brilliant of dramatic devices. The Play-scene is 'the climax and crisis of the whole drama'; and Shakespeare has performed a miracle in working into it everything that was necessary for the London audience, for the Elsinore audience, for Hamlet, for Claudius, for Polonius—each of whom needed something that the others did not. The London audience needed to know (the theory commits its author to believing that they could not otherwise have known) that the story of Gonzago was the same story as that of King Hamlet and Claudius. The Elsinore audience needed to know that Hamlet was plotting to kill his uncle. Hamlet needs to make Claudius reveal himself beyond question as the murderer of his brother; Claudius needs to be kept in the belief, which Hamlet had been shrewdly fostering, that his nephew's distemper is due to thwarted ambition; Polonius needs to be lulled with the old delusion about disprized love.

How Shakespeare not only built up this main arch of the play but also adorned it with 'a whole network of finer effects' is the subject of Dr Dover Wilson's fifth chapter, 'The Multiple Mouse-Trap'. One feature of it will strike every reader: that words which have hitherto been held too wild and whirling to have any meaning are shown to have clear dramatic force, and perhaps not one meaning merely but two, or even three, each aimed at a particular hearer. No one nowadays is likely to disagree with the suggestion of the double plane of vision offered by Shakespeare; the one for immediate apprehension, the other for reflection. For immediate apprehension Shakespeare was careful to provide a good strong story beyond which his groundlings would not trouble to press. To the more intelligent he offered subtler significances. It might be safe to add that now and then (and not in *Hamlet* only) he did not think of any section of his audience but wrote for himself, not caring whether or not anyone else would see all that he saw in his dialogue. It is not, then, an essential question whether the most intelligent among the spectators could have caught, in the theatre at a first, a second, a third hearing—even with a company rehearsed by Shakespeare himself—all that Dr Dover Wilson has found in years of study. Swept along on the swift and limpid waters of argument and interpretation, with the sun shining down on him and the wind behind him, the reader passes from joy to joy of discovery. And in thinking back over the voyage he is bound to admit that the whole thing (including the new suggestion of a blunder on the players' part and Hamlet's fury threat) hangs together: that the scene is both dramatically thrilling and of cardinal value to the plot: and that every line and word in it now bears, without distortion or supersubtle ingenuity, a meaning that helps the play.

It is in the fourth act, according to some, that *Hamlet* falls to pieces. Hamlet has lost his chance of killing the King; we know now that he never will until it is time for the play to end. The Prince himself is not seen; and the dramatist has somehow to fill up the time till he can fetch him back. The fourth act, according to Dr Dover Wilson, is cunningly contrived to keep Hamlet steadily before us by showing the tragic consequences of his inaction and by contrasting it with the way of Laertes—that truculent and treacherous bully whom only one so generous as Hamlet could mistake for 'a very noble youth'. Dramatically, it is time that Hamlet was taken back into our affections—time that he should stand again, if we may put it so, where he stood when he said, 'For my own poor part, Look you, I will go pray'. We must be shown again all that is appealing, noble, generous, and also strong and capable in a hero who for two acts has been savage, cruel, indolent, and futile. And the plot requires also that he should be the same Hamlet as he was when he failed to kill the King, and the same Hamlet as he was when he followed the Ghost and when he killed, like a rat, one whom he believed to be the King. In this new vision of the play the fourth act and the first part of the fifth are seen to perform this dramatic function perfectly, and without any straining or betrayal of the truth of character and incident. In other words, the dramatic mould is filled with consummate art, and the spectator's thoughts and feelings are guided with gentle mastery.

The interpretation involves the matter of Hamlet's sanity.

In the making of Hamlet... Shakespeare's task was not to produce a being psychologically explicable or consistent, but one who would evoke the affection, the wonder, and the tears of his audience, and would yet be accepted as entirely human.

It is clear, then, that anyone who asks Dr Dover Wilson for a precise diagnosis will get a dusty answer. He will be advised rather to study the 'antic disposition', and to see what Hamlet in the plot gained by being able to be taken for a madman, and what the play gained from the quibbles and other fantastic talk with which he encouraged the idea that he was mad. Hamlet was not mad to the extent of not being responsible for his actions and thus ceasing to be a hero and forfeiting 'our sympathy, our admiration—and our censure'. Nor was he so sane that the audience could think mere idleness or cowardice was the reason of his inaction. At moments he could be as crafty as Claudius and as violent as Laertes. Dr Dover Wilson can point to seven outbreaks of hysterical excitement (he is, perhaps, the first to show the intense dramatic force of the brutal outburst at the end of the Closet scene; and the attack on Laertes by Ophelia's grave is a reminder that Hamlet has not outgrown his 'sore distraction'). His study of melancholy as it was understood in Shakespeare's time leads him to a certain book, Timothy Bright's *Treatise of Melancholie,* which the play shows Shakespeare to have known. But there is no slavish following of any psychological theory. Hamlet's inaction was due to mental infirmity; but

Shakespeare, as every one knows, never furnishes an explanation for Hamlet's inaction. All he does is to exhibit it to us as a problem, turning it round and round, as it were, before our eyes so that we may see every side of it, and then in the end leaving us to draw our own conclusions—

and to realize how the aim of a great imaginative work of art has been achieved by the joy and the sorrow we have felt in its course.

There is mystery in *Hamlet.* But this book—a book which, be this or that in it right or wrong, must start for every one who reads it a new era in the understanding of the play— proves that the cause of the mystery is not dramatic incompetence in the author of this 'artistic masterpiece...perhaps the most successful piece of dramatic illusion the world has ever known'. Nor is the mystery due to psychological ignorance, to the presentation of a mind and character so ill defined that each player must put into the part what the author was unable to provide. It is the mystery of 'the faulty composition of man'; and when the mystery of *Hamlet* has been solved the mystery of human life will have been solved.

JOHN FLETCHER
(1925)

When Francis Beaumont, some three years married, died in 1616 at little over thirty years old, he had already ceased writing for the stage, it is supposed, for two or three years. His friend, housemate and collaborator, John Fletcher, had a decade and more of work without him before his body, caught and killed by the plague, was buried in St Saviour's, Southwark, on 29 August 1625. He made such good use of his time that his fame outsoared Beaumont's. It came to be hinted that Beaumont's part in the joint work had been that of a drag upon the wheels of Fletcher's genius, a steadying hand on the rein of his Pegasus. The injustice of that notion is too plain to any modern reader of *The Maid's Tragedy* or of *Philaster* to need comment now. Perhaps a greater injustice to both poets, caused by heedlessness of another kind, was that of a succeeding age, which thought of Beaumont and Fletcher as we should say Castor and Pollux or Liddell and Scott: conjoint and inseparable. Beaumont and Fletcher had been published, and very carelessly published, in a book during the days when men, having no playhouses to go to, were eager to read plays; and, the traditions and records about their separate achievements being allowed to lie unheeded, Beaumont and Fletcher became the author of all the fifty-two plays in the second folio. Of recent years scholarship, with its 'scientific' as well as its literary methods, in the labours of Fleay, of Boyle, of Bullen, perhaps especially of G. C. Macaulay, has gone a long way towards definitely separating Beaumont from Fletcher, and Fletcher from Beaumont, from Massinger, from Shakespeare, and from others with whom he collaborated; so that now, more clearly perhaps even than in his own time, we can see what sort of poet John Fletcher is.

John Fletcher

In spite of the absolutists in criticism, he is a poet whose work cannot be valued apart from his age and his origin. A dramatic poet is always more likely than any other sort of poet to be affected by the general conditions of his age; and Fletcher's origin may have helped to give practical effect to his great dramatic talent. He could have been—indeed, he was—a very fine lyric poet; but there was no livelihood in lyrical poetry, and Fletcher was in the unusual position of being a gentleman making a livelihood out of literature. His father was an odd mixture of the servile courtier and the fanatical Calvinist. By his handsome face, his engaging manners, his ruthless behaviour to Mary Stuart (at whose execution he acted chaplain) Richard Fletcher climbed in Elizabeth's graces as high as the Bishopric of London, only to fall, almost immediately, through theological excess and a second marriage with a rich widow of tarnished reputation. It is a pardonable fancy that sees in more than one of John Fletcher's loose Court ladies some memory of his stepmother. When his father died, leaving a large family and many debts, John was only seventeen years old; not too young in those days to have seen something of life at Court, and at least so born and bred as to have familiar access to those noblemen and gentlemen whose talk and manners his plays show him, and Dryden recorded him, to know very well. He cannot have been entirely without another gift from his father: the Puritanical view of life which, when imposed upon childhood, leads times without number to an adult view of life which is only Puritanism turned upside down.

The conditions of his age were at hand to encourage him in this view of life and to welcome its expression. Those conditions have often been described. It was the age of King James I: the age in which the great Elizabethan spirit, very nearly wrecked in the last years of the old Queen's reign, sailed into smooth water. It was an age in which men felt, first of all, the necessity of 'keeping it up'. They felt as men do in the first hours or days after completing some great and exciting task. They felt lassitude and aimlessness, and therewith restlessness. There was nothing very much to do, but repose seemed impossible. There was no great national enemy (and Walter Ralegh was to lose his head). There was no great Sovereign to be honourably feared or nobly hated or passionately loved; and for personal and national loyalty men must substitute (King James completely approving) the hothouse loyalty of an Amintor or an Archas. Even the mere pride and joy of living had paled; and here more than anywhere was there need of keeping it up. In drama Fletcher was a master of the art of keeping it up.

Drama, more quickly sensitive then than now (being then still the natural expression of the public spirit and not an artificially nurtured exercise in literature), responded swiftly to the growing separation between the plain man and the man of means and education; and James had done his share in the change by making court-servants of the players. John Fletcher, left at seventeen with half his father's books as his patrimony, must have found very early that he had a gift for writing the sort of play that was coming into fashion. He was probably not more than twenty-five, and was still to be taken into association by Beaumont, when he had already made his name in comedy. By the time he was thirty he had written (it is almost certain) *The Faithful Shepherdess* and *Monsieur Thomas* and *Woman's Prize*; and before he was thirty-five he had collaborated with Beaumont in *Four Plays*, *The Maid's Tragedy*, and *A King and No King*, besides writing his own *Valentinian* and *Bonduca* and *Wit Without Money*. He won favour quickly, and he kept it, not unbroken, indeed, but with no founderings like Ben Jonson's, because he knew what his public wanted. He had nothing in him of a Ben Jonson, labouring to force upon a stupid public what he knew was good for it, nor of an Ibsen following his own light through years of neglect and contempt, nor even of a Bernard Shaw, shrewdly discerning that the tide was almost at ebb and would soon turn. Fletcher was so much a man of his age that, with very few exceptions, he delighted the public by catching its taste at the very moment. It is well known how Beaumont and he brought back romance to the stage (and therein perhaps repaid to the Shakespeare of *The Winter's Tale* and *Cymbeline* and *The Tempest* certain debts which Beaumont at least had owed to the Shakespeare of the earlier comedies), and how they mingled romance with serious and even tragic matter, so that in the eyes of a time which had little fine fervour in itself romance took on the air of being real life and filled the gap of which most men were uneasily conscious. It is now well known, too, how true a poet and how fine a dramatist was Beaumont. But to get at Fletcher himself it is best perhaps to confine the attention to the plays which modern scholarship believes him to have written unaided. There may be thirteen of them in all; there may be as many as fifteen, or as few as eleven—on any count enough to judge by. Among them are, for certain, *The Faithful Shepherdess*, one of the few immediately unsuccessful things that he ever wrote, and perhaps the best; the tragedies of *Valentinian* and *Bonduca*, three or four good comedies, and some five of those 'tragi-comedies' to which Fletcher himself gave a peculiar turn.

The reason why modern readers find *The Faithful Shepherdess* the most beautiful of Fletcher's dramatic works is not only that it is the least straitly knit up with the Jacobean spirit (genius and even talent can keep the spirit of one age interesting to all that follow it); not only that it is the most fantastic and the most poetic by profession (the tragi-comedies are full as unlike real life, and there is poetry as good in several of them). Nor, for certain, is it that Fletcher is here using a form of dramatic verse, regular and strictly moulded, which, so far as is known, he never tried elsewhere.

> Fairest virgin, do not fear
> Me, that do thy body bear
> Not to hurt, but healed to be.
> Men are ruder far than we.
> See, fair goddess, in the wood
> They have let out yet more blood.
> Some savage man hath struck her breast
> So soft and white that no wild beast

Durst ha' touched asleep or 'wake:
So sweet, that adder, newt, or snake
Would have lain from arm to arm
On her bosom, to be warm
All a night, and being hot
Gone away and stung her not.
Quickly clap herbs to her breast;
A man sure is a kind of beast.

Thus the gentle, friendly Satyr speaks in the four-beat lines that were not unknown to the author of *L'Allegro*; and here is the graver note of the mourning shepherdess, Clorin:

Now no more shall these smooth brows be girt
With youthful coronals, and lead the dance;
No more the company of fresh fair maids
And wanton shepherds be to me delightful,
Nor the shrill pleasing sound of merry pipes
Under some shady dell, when the cool wind
Plays on the leaves: all be far away,
Since thou art far away; by whose dear side
How often have I sat crown'd with fresh flowers
For summer's queen, whilst every shepherd's boy
Puts on his lusty green, with gaudy hook
And hanging scrip of finest cordevan,
But thou art gone, and these are gone with thee,
And all are dead but thy dear memory;
That shall outlive thee and shall ever spring
Whilst there are pipes, or jolly shepherds sing.

To hear either note, or that of the passion-ridden shepherds and shepherdesses who play out their feverish parts, is to know that we are in the presence of a poet. Nothing in it is more remarkable than the ease. Now and then we find extravagance like this:

She's gone, she's gone! Blow high, thou north-west wind,
And raise the sea to mountains; let the trees
That dare oppose thy raging fury leese
Their firm foundation; creep into the earth
And shake the world, as at the monstrous birth
Of some new prodigy;

a particular instance which may be regarded either as looking back to Kyd or as opening the door (and Fletcher opened

several such doors) to the absurdities of Restoration tragedy.
But *The Faithful Shepherdess* has in it very little strain, very
little showing off. In telling his dramatic story the poet is
content to be simple in all his moods, so that when the Satyr
sings of the dawn:

> Now the birds begin to rouse,
> And the squirrel from the boughs
> Leaps to get him nuts and fruit;
> The early lark, that erst was mute,
> Carols to the rising day
> Many a note and many a lay,

we feel that this particular sort of simplicity is dramatic,
indeed, but not affected. There is hot-house work in the play,
it is true. The inverted Puritan in Fletcher peeps out of his
eyes when he looks at chastity and at passion. But only here
and in one or two of the comedies do we feel that the poet was
writing with conviction, and with no care about what is now
called the box-office.

Not even *Bonduca* can be excepted from that statement. It
is not pedantry that would deny to *Valentinian* the title of
tragedy. The rape by a lascivious tyrant of his greatest general's
wife might make a good starting-point for a tragedy; but it is
no tragedy that includes the grotesque sufferings of the Emperor under poison (all the more grotesque for being introduced
by one of the loveliest of Fletcher's lovely songs, 'Care-
charming sleep'); and it is no tragedy that has for 'hero' such
a character as the outraged woman's husband is turned into
by the need of a climax. Indeed, is there anything feebler in
Elizabethan drama (which could be as feeble as it could be
mighty) than the soliloquy of Maximus in the third scene of
the fifth act? His wife has killed herself; he has killed not only
her ravisher but his own best friend, Aecius, who would have
stood in his way. Now he will nobly die himself on the ruin
and the void that he has made. At least, so he begins by saying.
And then suddenly comes this:

> And now, Aecius and my honoured Lady,
> That were preparers to my rest and quiet,

> The lines to lead me to Elysium....
> First smile upon the sacrifice I have sent ye,
> Then see me coming boldly: stay; I am foolish,
> Somewhat too sudden to mine own destruction,
> This great end of my vengeance may grow greater;
> Why may I not be Caesar? Yet no dying!

If this be not Fletcher's supposed vice of 'huddling up' the ends of his plays, he had not that vice. But it is due to a worse vice than mere 'huddling-up', Sheridan-wise, while the players were waiting. It brings us face to face with a weakness which is prominent in nearly all Fletcher's more serious work and some of his comic work. A play had become little more than a minister of sensation; it had ceased to be an expression of vitality. Maximus must turn Emperor only because out of his marriage with Valentinian's widow and his spectacular murder by that suddenly useful dummy another ounce of sensation may be squeezed. From bungling and absurdity of this kind *Bonduca* is free. It deserves to be called a tragedy. In Caratach it has a true hero: in little Hengo, his nephew, one of the most natural and winning of play-children; in Bonduca's younger daughter's dread of the suicide which honour compels her to commit, a wringing touch of Euripidean truth. And yet one cannot shake off uneasiness. It is one thing to play ducks and drakes with the characters of two Romans, Junius and Petillius, so as to get more surprises into the action. It is another and a worse thing to fill Caratach, the noblest Briton of them all, the man who was fighting, and would go on fighting to the last drop of his blood, against his country's foes, with the 'sportsmanlike' notions of a duellist, who for the sake of 'honour' will give advantages to his enemy. This, more than Caratach's 'huddled-up' surrender over the dead boy's body at the close, is the cause of one's suspicion that Fletcher did not know what tragedy was because he lacked the high seriousness that alone can make it. To Caratach, tragic hero, he gives sentiments that seem a little absurd even in Demetrius, the hero of a tragi-comedy.

On the face of it tragi-comedy is a bastard form. Fletcher's own definition of it leaves it a thing of compromise and artifice:

> A tragi-comedy is not so called in respect of mirth and killing, but in respect it wants deaths, which is enough to make it no tragedy, yet brings some near it, which is enough to make it no comedy.

And just because it was a thing of compromise and artifice Fletcher did in it some of his best work and some of his worst work. If we were introducing Fletcher's drama to one who knew nothing of it, we should put into his hands *The Humorous Lieutenant*, a play which rouses delight at a first reading and at the twentieth. Here is all Fletcher in one play: the best of his mind in brave Celia; in her lover, the gallant, hot-headed Demetrius; in blunt, kindly old Leontius the soldier; and in the whimsically droll Lieutenant, who is a lion when he is ill and a lazy coward when he is well; and in Celia's temptation by lewd old King Antigonus (a favourite subject with Fletcher) enough of the worst of his mind to be a warning of what will be found elsewhere. Here is the best of his work: in the fine eloquence of Demetrius and of Celia; in the natural, rugged talk of Leontius; in such exciting scenes as those in which Celia mocks or outfaces Antigonus, or rounds upon Demetrius for suspecting her honour; such pathetic scenes as the parting between the lovers; such scenes of pure comedy as their meeting after their quarrel, and old Leontius's fatherly wheedling of them into reconciliation. And for a taste of the most careless of Fletcher's work here we find him, after he has built up his play in scene after scene, each seeming better than the last, and each adroitly made to forward and heighten the action, suddenly 'huddling-up' the end as tamely as a modern musical comedy. It must be admitted that *The Humorous Lieutenant* has a peculiar charm, for Celia is the most delightful girl in all Fletcher. She expresses dramatically the best of that 'feminism' which peeps out argumentatively in other plays—*The Pilgrim*, for instance, *The Woman's Prize*, and *The Wild Goose Chase*—a snatching at what women could be, which contrasts very oddly with a score of representations in Fletcher

of what he sometimes felt that they were. This was but part
of the sickness of soul from which he made Memnon, the mad
lover in the play of that name, a notable sufferer: the Puritanical sickness which hates the body, hates passion and hates
woman. Fletcher, no thinker, was at the mercy of his
impulses; and his aims were those of the craftsman, not the
artist. His care was how to screw out a little more and yet a
little more sensation. And that led him, in tragi-comedy,
the form where he was most at home, to write, late in life,
A Wife for a Month. There is no need to dwell upon it.
It deserves all the hardest things that Coleridge or another
ever said of Fletcher's morality. But the saddest thing of
all about it is that to-day it shows itself not only wicked but
absurd.

After it the comedies seem but wholesomely coarse. They
are full of invention, some of it very happily farcical; and the
simply seen characters are always nicely arranged for conflict
and reaction. Except here and there, they lack the fineness of
comic vision and the choiceness of comic expression which
came after the Restoration and the Revolution; but they are
great fun in their rough-and-tumble wit. Most agreeable of
all to-day is *Monsieur Thomas,* because travelled Tom himself
—all prunes and prism to his old father who would have him
be a rake, and the wildest of gay dogs to his betrothed who
wants him to settle down and behave nicely—is even more
whimsically droll a fellow than the humorous lieutenant himself, and with a firmer foundation in purpose. This, too, is
almost the only comedy of Fletcher's in which there is no call
to put up with sparks who to modern taste seem cads. Considering what Jonson had done to these gallants, it is surprising
that Fletcher should go on holding up to admiration his
Valentines, his Mirabels, and such. But Fletcher was no
satirist, and he was a man of his time; and the gallants of
Tudor and Stuart times, as we see them in literature, are cads.

As craftsman, then, he can do whatever he has a mind to do.
And he invented for his purpose an instrument by which his
hand can be traced, almost for certain, wherever it lit. That

lissom line, with its redundant syllables, its 'feminine' endings, its obvious definition by stress and not by scansion; the observance of a line as in itself a period, which to Leslie Stephen's ear produced 'a sing-song that tires by its monotony', but might claim to be a very serviceable calculation of what the actor's breath and tongue could compass; the way in which, by parenthesis and added clause and other devices, the meaning seems to think itself out, the emotion to come to consciousness, in the character even while he is speaking—these are unmistakable signs of Fletcher and of his deliberate attempt as craftsman to forge a new thing, which is verse to look at, but in essence so much rather mere dramatic speech that he never had need to use prose. To study the efficiency of it, the variety with which he can use it, and the positive achievements in eloquence (perhaps *The Island Princess* is his masterpiece in this respect), in the shimmering play of comic dialogue, in any mode that he chooses, is to realize that, as craftsman, he was fit to collaborate with Shakespeare (not merely, as has been sometimes supposed, to finish off what Shakespeare had discarded), and that he, indeed, and no other, wrote Wolsey's farewell. Some minds will always feel a little reluctance in accepting that association, because Fletcher as artist was immeasurably beneath Fletcher as craftsman. Let us believe that the success of Beaumont and Fletcher, rather than any profound psychological development, turned Shakespeare to the writing of the last romances; and still there is no missing the quality of what he put into them. He had something he wanted to say. Fletcher never had anything he wanted to say. He knew what the public wanted. His is artifice cut loose from any belief or conviction. The result is that in reading him one is never free from the discomfort of his cleverness. That is the stuff to give them!—and how skilfully he gives it them! And at his best how shrewdly, no matter at what cost to right thinking, or to the truth, not only of life itself but of the postulates and the logic of his own play, he will give just one more turn to the screw of sensation! At all costs, let us go on keeping it up!

But this is no note to end upon when tercentenaries are being celebrated. Here is a better:

> Away delights, go seek some other dwelling,
>> For I must dye:
> Farewel false Love, thy tongue is ever telling
>> Lye after Lye.
> For ever let me rest now from thy smarts.
>> Alas, for pity go,
>> And fire their hearts
> That have been hard to thee, mine was not so.

Whatever his lack, he was a true poet in his songs. He wrote *Hence, all you vain delights*, which Milton made the mother of *Il Penseroso*. He wrote *Come hither, you that love*, and *God Lyaeus, ever young*. Very likely he wrote *Orpheus with his lute*.

THOMAS DEKKER AND
THE UNDERDOG
(1941)

In what year did Thomas Dekker die? Nobody knows. The weight of conjecture favours 1632. Sir Edmund Chambers inclines to identify him with the Thomas Decker who was buried at St James's, Clerkenwell, on 25 August 1632; and Dr Greg, in the first number of the *Modern Language Review* (1906), went so far as to say that 'his death occurred the year of the publication of the *Six Court Comedies*, which was 1632. A. W. Ward, following Fleay, chose 1632. But 1641 has its supporters. In the admirable old eleventh edition of the *Encyclopaedia Britannica* Minto and McKerrow are committed to it. In the *Dictionary of National Biography* Bullen suggested it. In the *Cambridge History of English Literature*, Vol. v favours 1637, but Vol. vi proposes 1641. That year, then, has authority in plenty for anyone who wants to write about Dekker but thinks it only decent to pretend to some excuse. And since Dekker is an exceptionally inviting Elizabethan to write about, and his admirers always want to win him new admirers, let us suppose that in this 1941 of ours falls the three hundredth anniversary of his death.

During the greater part of his working life he was a writer of plays; and as he wrote much and quickly, nearly always in collaboration and very often as a reviser of others' work, and since the Elizabethan and Jacobean drama has a way of edging every other kind of contemporary literature out of the picture, very much of what has been written about Dekker has been concerned with those teasing problems of dramatic history, those attempts to disentangle the threads of authorship in the composite plays, which distract a reader's attention, perhaps, too often from the quality and virtue of the finished work.

95

Thomas Dekker and the Underdog

If newcomers to Dekker could be advised to take no notice of his plays until they had got to know him well from his other works, they might respond the more readily to his indubitable touch when they recognized it in a play. Dekker's prose is a manifold joy. Dekker's lyric verse is among the best of its period. But hack dramatist and clumsy constructor though he was, he soars in the plays to heights unknown in his other work; and the full beauty of his mind and hand cannot be told without a knowledge of certain plays that are all his own, and of one or two that are composite. The prose and the lyrics, therefore, make a convenient approach.

From 1603 to 1609, while there was something of a lull in his theatre work, Dekker wrote about a dozen prose pamphlets. His first, *The Batchelars Banquet*, was a translation from the French, and is among the very best examples of the Tudor art of translation; but the authentic and original Dekker is first found in another pamphlet, *The Wonderfull Yeare*, 1603. It was the year of the death of Queen Elizabeth and the accession of King James I. Dekker begins by describing the English spring as English writers have always liked to describe it—in raptures about its balmy beauty as far from the truth as the Arcadian simplicity and merriment of the shepherds and their wenches. The reader will not fail to observe that, unlike most of these humbugging rhapsodists, Dekker brings the spring into the town, where the necessary olives and palms get a faint suggestion of verisimilitude by being planted at men's doors and carried in their hands; and, when he has worked the whole sham effect up to its height in 'heauen lookt like a Pallace, and the great hall of the earth like a Paradice', he suddenly shows his hand. A storm arises. Before we can draw breath, we are on the real earth and in the real England, none the less actual for being very ornamentally described. Queen Elizabeth falls sick and dies. There is consternation, not in Arcady, but in England. Shepherds, indeed, droop for the loss of their goddess; but the true consternation is among courtiers, lawyers, merchants and citizens, real and worthy men; and the usurers and brokers, 'that are

96

the Diuels Ingles, and dwell in the long lane of hell', quake like aspen leaves for fear of the maimed old soldiers, who now bristle up the quills of their stiff porcupine mustachios, and swear that now was the hour come for them to stir their stumps.

Loose-limbed, rapid verse is called in to help describe the universal dismay and disorder on the removal of her who had 'brought up (euen under her wing) a nation that was almost begotten and borne under her'. Then suddenly this 'Protean Climactericall yeare hath metamorphosed himselfe' into another shape. King James I ascends the throne. The universal joy is described with equal elaboration and ornament, but with equal attention to real men and callings— courtiers, soldiers, scholars, tailors, smiths, even players' boys. But once more our lavish author has whirled us up only to dash us down with the greater force. He has come to the subject for the sake of which all that went before was written.

The wonderful year of King James's accession was also the year of a very bad plague; and all that Pepys, all that even Defoe had to say about the plague of 1665 is pale and trifling compared with Dekker's account of London in the plague of 1603. He begins it with a ghastly description of a charnel-house (one of many things in his works which suggest that he knew his Shakespeare pretty well). Even such a formidable shape did the diseased city appear in. Generous and precise with detail, but relying very little on the merely disgusting, he forces the horror, the mystery, the loneliness and emptiness of it all upon our senses:

For he that durst (in the dead houre of gloomy midnight) haue bene so valiant, as to haue walkt through the still and melancholy streets, what thinke you should haue bene his musicke? Surely the loud grones of rauing sicke men; the strugling panges of soules departing: In euery house griefe striking up an Allarum: Seruants crying out for maisters: wiues for husbands, parents for children, children for their mothers: here he should haue met some frantickly running to knock up Sextons; there, others fearfully sweating with Coffins, to steale forth dead bodies, least the fatall handwriting of death should seale up their doores. And to make this dismall consort more full, round about him Bells heauily tolling in one place, and ringing out in another.

The moment comes when his spirit grows faint with rowing in this Stygian ferry; and he turns to yarning, telling tales tragic, or tragically comic, of actual persons and events. Many of these pages strike home to the business and bosom of any who may read them to-day. They concern refugees.

Twenty-two years later, at the other extreme of his activity as pamphleteer, Dekker wrote about another plague. The accession of King Charles I, like that of his father, was marked by a bad (by a very much worse) plague, the plague, notorious in theatrical history, of 1625. The difference between the two pamphlets is very wide. The old man is heartbroken.

O London! (thou Mother of my Life, Nurse of my being) a hard-hearted sonne might I be counted, if here I should not dissolue all into teares, to heare thee powring forth thy passionate condolements.

His style is much simpler; his grief strikes deep into the reader's emotion, leaving the senses less harrowed. The plague is sincerely accepted as the wages of sin, and the moralizing of the earlier pamphlet becomes conventional by comparison. The pamphlet of 1625 was meant as 'A Rod for Run-awayes'. It is addressed to 'the Reader that flyes, the Reader that stayes, the Reader lying in a Haycocke, the hard-hearted Country-Reader, and the broken-hearted City-Reader'. The parallel with our own day is far from exact; but some, at least, of the moral may come home to us. The rich runaways have deserted London. They have left their beautiful houses to emptiness and degradation. They have left the poor to destitution without their wonted charity; and away in their safe retreats they are eating up all the food that ought to be coming into London. Once more Dekker lightens the burden of woe by turning to tales of refugees, and of hardhearted countrymen who resented their coming; but nothing could go far to allaying the awe and sadness he has induced by his description—much more economical than that of the earlier work—of the loneliness in the echoing city streets and churches, the misery, the destitution and the terror.

Certain qualities will be already evident in him. He is a Londoner in spirit as well as by birth and nurture. He is a realist; no matter how Nashe-like and flowery his language may be, he keeps his eye and his mind steadily on what is actually before him. And he is tender-hearted, with a great pity for the poor and no small contempt and hatred for the selfish and the oppressor. These are the three qualities which, not always in perfect agreement, shine in all his prose works. A fourth might possibly be detected—a missionary love of virtue; but even when Dekker is at his most didactic, as in *The Seuen Deadly Sinnes of London* (1606), he is keener on describing the actually prevalent workaday London offences against honest trading, family affection and so forth than on the reformation of his readers. In *The Belman of London* (1608) and its sequel, *Lanthorne and Candle-light* (1609), he discourses, as Awdelay, Harman and Greene had done before him, of rogues, their orders, their tricks and their language; and however virtuously shocked he may appear, he is mightily interested and curious about these slices of real life.

Dekker begins *The Belman* with a rhapsody on the beauty of the country and the simplicity of life there—an innocently obvious trick to heighten the effect of the rowdy den of thieves that he found in a sylvan retreat and the foul crone who, in drink, told him all about them. In the famous *Guls Hornebooke* (1609) he shows a power of observation of things below the surface. It is because he has detected the reason why the coffee-houses, playhouses, bawdy houses of London are thronged by so many young, swaggering (as we should say now) bounders that he can make his gull show himself off throughout a typical London day. The Londoner and the realist are, perhaps, nowhere in Dekker's work so plain as they are in this withering guide for gulls. There is little sign of the tender heart. But then the gulls had money; they belonged to the ruling class. It was the underdog that had Dekker's heart. The motto of his *Worke for Armorours* (1609) is 'God helpe the Poore, The rich can shift'. And there is good excuse for wondering whether this is really an early Jacobean author who, at a bear-baiting, pities the crushed dogs and the whipped and bleeding bear, and goes on:

> Methought this whipping of the blinde Beare, moued as much pittie in my breast towards him, as the leading of poore starued wretches to the whipping posts in London (when they had more neede to be releeued with foode) ought to moue the hearts of Citizens, though it be the fashion now to laugh at the punishment.

Gratiano, we are prepared to believe, was a gentleman compared with some who saw him on the stage of the Globe or even of the Blackfriars; but who is this who is sorry for the bear?

For all that, he could not honestly have maintained that his only pleasure in the spectacle lay in his reflection that the dogs driven to the attack were 'a liuely representation of poore men going to lawe with the rich and mightie', or that the old ape on horseback suggested 'the infortunate condition of Soldiers' (Dekker had much admiration and pity for soldiers), 'and old seruitors...compeld to follow the heeles of Asses with gay trappings'. It is well to realize that Dekker's insatiable interest in the exuberant popular London life of his day was too strong sometimes for his compassion. It will prevent our being shocked if we find ourselves convinced that in *The Honest Whore* he wrote the scene at Bethlem Monastery (Bedlam) in the first part and the scene at Bridewell in the second part, as well as the noblest oddities of old Friscobaldo, the loveliest things set down for unperverted Hippolito and for reformed Bellafront, and the famous, Portia-like speech of Candido, the patient man:

> Patience my Lord: why tis the soule of peace:
> Of all the vertues tis neer'st kin to heaven.
> It makes men looke like gods: the best of men
> That ere wore earth about him, was a sufferer,
> A soft, meeke, patient, humble, tranquill spirit,
> The first true Gentleman that ever breath'd.

Thomas Dekker and the Underdog

Bedlam and Bridewell were, after all, sights of London town; and Dekker was proud of them.

The lines just quoted are evidence that a good deal of play-writing in a hurry had not spoiled Dekker's hand at blank verse. He could write loosely and verbosely; and most of the poetry in *Dekker His Dreame* (1620), a rhapsody (mainly in verse), in which he strove his hardest to realize Heaven and Hell, shows that the more he strained after effect the less he succeeded. He could pile it on to any extent in prose, but not in verse. But his many beauties in blank verse (with the frequent and well-placed snatches of rhyme in it) and his failures elsewhere only heighten the desire to know all about his lyric poetry. Every one knows the poem *Art thou poor, yet hast thou golden slumbers?* which the old basket-weaver Janiculo sings in *Patient Grissill*, a play which Dekker wrote with Chettle and Haughton; and no one doubts that Dekker's it is. It is safe, too, to allow to Dekker the heart-breaking lullaby, *Golden slumbers kiss your eyes*, which, in that same maddening play, the old man sings to his two grand-children, when Grissill's 'noble' husband has turned them all out of doors. For his own play, *The Shoemakers' Holiday*, he wrote two songs for three men to sing. One is *O the month of Maie, the merrie month of Maie*, which more than any other Eliza-bethan spring song recalls Nashe's *Spring, the sweet Spring, is the year's pleasant king.* The other is a jolly drinking song (and, since song is always more timeless than prose, there is small harm in using modern spelling):

> Cold's the wind and wet's the rain,
> Saint Hugh be our good speed:—
> Ill is the weather that bringeth no gain,
> Nor helps good hearts in need.
> Troll the bowl, the jolly nut-brown bowl,
> And here, kind mate, to thee:
> Let's sing a dirge for Saint Hugh's soul,
> And down it merrily;

with more to the same effect, 'as often as there be men to drinke'. In other plays and royal or civic entertainments written undoubtedly by Dekker there are at least ten lyrics, not counting snatches. One of those in *Old Fortunatus* goes:

> Virtue's branches wither, Virtue pines;
> O pity, pity, and alack the time!
> Vice doth flourish, Vice in glory shines;
> Her gilded boughs above the cedar climb.
> Vice hath golden cheeks, O pity, pity!
> She in every land doth monarchize.
> Virtue is exiled from every city.
> Virtue is a fool, Vice only wise.
> O pity, pity, Virtue weeping dies.
> Vice laughs to see her faint (alack the time!)
> This sinks; with painted wings the other flies.
> Alack that best should fall, and bad should climb.
> O pity, pity, pity, mourn, not sing!
> Vice is a Saint, Virtue an underling.
> Vice doth flourish, Vice in glory shines:
> Virtue's branches wither, Virtue pines.

One more example must suffice. The song of the Cyclops from *London's Tempe* begins:

> Brave iron, brave hammer! from your sound
> The art of music has her ground;
> On the anvil thou keep'st time,
> Thy knick-a-knock is a smith's best chime.
>   Yet thwick-a-thwack.
>   Thwick, thwack-a-thwack, thwack,
>   Make our brawny sinews crack;
> Then pit-a-pat, pat, pit-a-pat, pat,
>   Till thickest bars be beaten flat.
>   We shoe the horses of the sun,
>   Harness the dragons of the moon....

As the song goes on he contrives to combine no little poetical fancy with the onomatopoeic nonsense. It is plain at first sight that the writer has command of ease and freedom of metrical movement, and that he knows very well how to write a lyric for singing by particular characters in particular circumstances. Here, indeed, are 'words-for-music', and the many repetitions are meant as a help to the composer. When, therefore, we find the same characteristics in the lyrics in plays where Dekker collaborated with some one else, we may

use these tests on them. In *Westward Ho!* he collaborated
with Webster; but in the final song:

> Oares, oares, oares, oares!
> To London hey, to London hey!
> Hoist up sails and lets away
> For the safest bay
> For us to land is London shores;

we have something very different from any lyric poetry that
Webster is known to have written, and scarcely need to recall
that Dekker is the poet who knew and loved the London
workers, watermen, apprentices and what not. When we
come upon *The Sun's Darling*, in which, late in his career,
Dekker collaborated with Ford, we find no fewer than eight
songs, all worthy of the most richly poetical play (or masque)
in the Dekker canon, all unlike any known song of Ford's,
and nearly all showing the lyrical characteristics of Dekker—
with a brave song of the haymakers, rakers, reapers and mowers
to head the list.

That opens up an exciting possibility. One of those songs,
What bird so sings, yet so does wail—a song in which our old
friends the nightingale and the cuckoo are joined, more
naturalistically than usual, with the lark and the sparrow—
had already appeared, in a slightly different form, in the *Six
Court Comedies*, by Lyly, of 1632, in which the songs to be
sung in those comedies were printed for the first time. *The
Sun's Darling*, though licensed for performance in 1624, was
not printed till 1656; and it was natural to suppose that the
1632 version of the song was earlier than the 1656 version.
Dr Greg, in the article referred to above, showed excellent
reason for recognizing that the 1632 was a revised and
trimmed version of the rougher, very obviously words-for-
music version of 1656. No question but that the version in
The Sun's Darling is very like Dekker. But if he wrote one
of the songs first found in that 1632 edition of Lyly's comedies
did he write all the others? They have only been ascribed to
Lyly because they appeared in that volume, published twenty-
six years after Lyly's death. Was Dekker, not Lyly nor any

other, the poet who wrote *Cupid and my Campaspe played*, and *My shag-hair cyclops* (which has its affinities with the 'Brave iron' of *London's Tempe*), and the song about Daphne, and the hymns to Apollo and to Cupid? Here, indeed, would be justification for Lamb's remark that Dekker had 'poetry enough for anything'.

Lamb was not thinking only or chiefly of the lyrical poetry. 'His smallest scraps of song are bewitching', said another critic; but, on the whole, it would be better to know Dekker's plays without knowing his prose and his songs than the other way round. An interesting course, as we have tried to suggest, is to approach the plays by way of the pamphlets and the songs, because they prepare the reader to recognize in this hard-working, ill-rewarded hack the soul of a pure poet with a passion for beauty, especially for moral beauty, for loving-kindness, gaiety of spirit and chaste and faithful love. Cruelty, oppression and selfishness make him rather sad than angry. He is no foe to just authority; but tyranny—of parents over their children, or of convention and ignorance over poor old women, called witches—he cannot stomach. In construction and episode he can be almost childish; but in spirit he never goes wrong, whether he is flooding middle-class London life with the radiance of happy good will, or showing the agonies of remorse, or soaring to ethereal heights of religious aspiration. And so to *The Shoemakers' Holiday* and *Old Fortunatus* and *The Honest Whore*, and the fun of looking for the Dekker touch in *Patient Grissill*, *The Witch of Edmonton*, *The Sun's Darling* and *The Virgin Martyr*.

WILLIAM CONGREVE

(1929)

When Congreve died (two hundred years ago next Saturday) he was mourned by his old schoolfellow Swift, who said he had loved him from his youth, and by another lifelong friend, Sir Richard Temple (Lord Cobham), and by Pope and Steele and Prior and Rowe and Addison and Gay and others of the Augustan men of letters, who were to miss not only the wit and scholarship but the simplicity and urbanity of one of 'the three most honest-hearted real good men of the poetical members' of the Kit-Cat Club. He was buried in Westminster Abbey, and his pall was borne by four peers of the realm. But his grand friend and patroness, Henrietta Duchess of Marlborough, caused an image of him to be made and set it up at her table. Round the feet were cloths, just as there had been round the gouty feet of the living poet. On the body were the poet's clothes, and on the head his wig—all, we may be sure, of his most splendid. But there was no need now for the hat, which he had been used to wear low over his brows, to guard his eyes from the light and his thoughts from prying neighbours. The purblind eyes were quite blind now. It seems a very strange freak of the great lady. Mr Congreve life-size, but without Mr Congreve's wit and charm, and without Mr Congreve's vision—she was pampering not so much her grief as its reputation. And yet what the Duchess of Marlborough then did is pretty much what criticism has been doing ever since. It has set up an image of Congreve and treated it as if it were the poet. Those bandaged feet are the coarseness and immorality of the comedy of his day. His splendid clothes and imposing wig are the airs and graces of the society about which he wrote and of the manner in which he wrote about it. And the eyes are blind because it has rarely occurred to anyone to inquire how far Congreve did actually see into truth, and what his vision showed him. No critic, not even Hazlitt wholly, has treated that image for the dummy that it is—until our own day. In 1924 two things happened which combined to start a new era in the estimation of Congreve's comedies. One was the public production at the Lyric Theatre, Hammersmith, of *The Way of the World*, which, though previously staged by theatrical societies and at the Maddermarket Theatre, Norwich, then first for two centuries (and perhaps in all its existence), had its full chance of being judged as a stage-play, and proved Hazlitt right about its merit under that head. The other event was the publication of Mr Bonamy Dobrée's book, *Restoration Comedy*. One would suspect some secret link of sympathy between Congreve's mind and Mr Dobrée's. Agreeing with a remark of Hazlitt's about *The Way of the World*, he writes of Hazlitt's 'faculty of seeing more clearly than any of his contemporaries'. He has seen farther than Hazlitt. To have been shown Mr Dobrée's Congreve is to see that the best thing to do with the dummy is to take it out and make a Guy Fawkes of it.

A la-di-da fine gentleman with several lucrative sinecures, brilliant, immoral, cynical, cold, who sported very elegantly in exquisite dialogue with the affectations and follies and appetites of smart men and women and their servants, fell into a huff because he got the worst of it in a controversy with a parson, and when his next play was not liked turned a superior back upon the drama for ever; that was the old idea of Congreve; and while his wit was always exalted, nothing else was found in him to praise. And there was always the wretched little anecdote about the visit of Voltaire, which has probably been mistold more often than any other anecdote:

> Having long conversed familiarly with the great, he wished to be considered rather as a man of fashion than of wit; and when he received a visit from Voltaire, disgusted him by the despicable foppery of desiring to be considered not as an author but a gentleman.

Thus Johnson, who might perhaps have been more careful or more just if Congreve had not been a Whig and a placeman.

Congreve was not so little a gentleman as to be so great a snob. His familiar friends were men of letters. And what Voltaire had written was this:

He spoke of his works as trifles that were beneath him, and hinted to me in our first conversation that I should visit him upon no other footing than that of a gentleman who led a life of plainness and simplicity.

And that was precisely what he then was: a gentleman (that is, a private person) leading that sort of life. He was old and ill. It was twenty-six years since the failure of *The Way of the World*; he wrote verses now, when he wrote at all, and only to please himself. The theatre was in other hands, and the stage occupied with other kinds of play. To these obvious good reasons why Congreve should not wish to discuss his plays with the busy French stranger Edmund Gosse added another: 'the indifference, the chagrin, of an aged man of letters, stricken with silence, with never a drop of ichor left in his shrunken vein'—a state of which Edmund Gosse had no personal experience. Behind and below all these may lie a still more cogent reason—the very same reason, perhaps, which induced him to give up writing plays. And if it is found to deserve the name of pride, it will certainly not prove to be the sort of pride at which Johnson roared and others have sneered. To Voltaire's final impertinence: 'I answered that had he been so unfortunate as to be a mere gentleman, I should never have come to see him', the milkmaid in the nursery rhyme of 'Where are you going to' could provide Congreve with the perfect reply, which he would have been too much of a gentleman to use.

To have discussed his plays with Voltaire would have been to open old wounds. And if, after twenty-six years, those wounds still shrank from being touched, it was not from any excessively sensitive self-conceit in the man himself. That he was more sensitive than the average man must be taken for granted: men of genius always are. He could show it, too, with a straightforward and wholesome petulance. His second play, *The Double-Dealer*, had not pleased the public in general.

It was too hard on the men: it was too hard on the women: it had too many soliloquies in it: these and many other reasons were given, the true one probably being that that audience did not like being confronted, in a comedy, with figures of wickedness so real, so raw, so devoid of all their own frivolity and carelessness as those of Maskwell and Lady Touchwood. Therefore in Congreve's next play Mr Scandal is given the famous outburst against the state of the poet, who must be 'more servile, timorous and fawning' than the basest of human creatures, 'without you could retrieve the ancient honours of the name, recall the stage of Athens, and be allowed the force of open, honest satire'. In that speech there is a good deal of sincere championship of the high office of poet: in the whole scene, with the servant taking his smart share (and did even Congreve, who created Lady Wishfort, ever write anything more brilliantly clever than his Jeremy's mixture of coarseness and refinement—unwashed but scented?), there is a great deal of personal pique. But, after all, there was some excuse. He was not yet twenty-four, an unknown youth from the country, when his first play was accepted by Davenant for the Theatre Royal, Drury Lane, hailed by Dryden with enthusiasm, and by the public with so much avidity that it saved the toppling fortunes of a theatre that seemed to be doomed. And more than that. Dryden, Southerne and Maynwaring touched up the play before its production; but it was not they, or any of them, who wrote:

Vainlove. Business must be followed, or be lost.

Bellmour. Business!—and so must time, my friend, be close pursued, or lost. Business is the rub of life, perverts our aim, casts off the bias, and leaves us wide and short of the intended mark.

Vain. Pleasure, I guess, you mean.

Bell. Ay, what else has meaning?

Vain. Oh, the wise will tell you—

Bell. More than they believe—or understand.

Vain. How, how, Ned, a wise man say more than he understands?

Bell. Ay, ay; wisdom's nothing but a pretending to know and believe more than we really do.

The noisy, inattentive audience of the day could hardly have taken in those, which were almost the first words of Congreve ever heard in the theatre; and, if they had, they could hardly have been expected to realize what had happened. But Dryden knew. And Congreve knew. And then, when *The Double-Dealer* failed, there came that poem from Dryden, the noblest and most moving declaration of faith and love which an old poet ever wrote to a young poet—or indeed perhaps one man ever wrote to another. And there was Swift's poem, too, as hot in rage against the glib, gossiping, belittling public as it was high in the admiration of one who believed himself a poetaster for one whom he knew to be a poet. When King Dryden names you as his son and successor, and Swift rails not at you but at your detractors, you may be excused for believing that your own consciousness of genius is well founded.

Whichever way Congreve turned, he found himself able to do better than most people. We must except, of course, most of his poems, especially those which he wrote after his disappointments in the theatre had made him afraid to be himself. But there was promise of better things in his youth. At twenty, or thereabouts, he wrote the irregular ode on 'Mrs Arabella Hunt, Singing'; and that beautiful thing, like some of his little songs, is the work of a poet, whereas any careful scholar could have shown that Pindar's odes were not irregular, and have written the two very dull examples which set English ode-writers in the right path. But there is no need to go outside the plays to see (now that Mr Dobrée has helped all to look fearlessly) the variety of Congreve's power. Let it be taken as demonstrated beyond question that 'his style is inimitable, nay perfect'. But he has more than one way of using his mastery over English words.

Lady Touchwood. Thunder strike thee dead for this deceit! immediate lightning blast thee, me, and the whole world!—Oh! I could rack myself, play the vulture to my own heart, and gnaw it piecemeal, for not boding to me this misfortune!
Mellefont. Be patient.
Lady Touch. Be damned!

Mel. Consider, I have you on the hook; you will but flounder yourself a-weary, and be nevertheless my prisoner.

Lady Touch. I'll hold my breath and die, but I'll be free.

Mel. O madam, have a care of dying unprepared. I doubt you have some unrepented sins that may hang heavy and retard your flight.

Lady Touch. Oh, what shall I do? Say? Whither shall I turn? Has hell no remedy?

Mel. None; hell has served you even as Heaven has done, left you to yourself.

It is horrible: the woman, a very wicked woman, cornered at last and really afraid; the man, with every excuse to be cruel, bantering the bitter enemy who is at last in his power. But the passionate tensity of that moment could be paralleled from *The Way of the World* in the ugly, snarling scene between Fainall and Mrs Marwood. And there is plenty of passion in *The Mourning Bride*, however slight the appeal to modern sympathies of these Oriental potentates and their wars and captives, and however clumsily the plot itself may come blundering through the reader's desire to be illuded. The third act, where the visits of the two women to the hero in prison lead up to the famous tag:

> Heaven has no rage like love to hatred turned,
> Nor hell a fury like a woman scorned,

is a fine piece of sustained and varied emotion, strong drama that seems to grow and not to be hammered out. More thrilling still is Zara's speech of apprehension at the silence of the prison where there used to be a dreadful din of groans and howls and chains and creaking hinges. And though Johnson fought Garrick 'with great ardour' to uphold his belief that Almeria's description of the temple surpassed anything in Shakespeare as 'a description of material objects, without any intermixture of moral notions', his defence was timorous. The description becomes all the finer when it is known why Almeria had gone to the temple at all. And Congreve could do pretty well when it came to moral notions. Almeria's speculations on the cause of human misery and Osmyn's on human reason and the

eternal justice may not go very deep, but they are not the work
of a trifler spinning smart remarks; and Almeria's reflection:

> But 'tis the wretch's comfort still to have
> Some small reserve of near and inward woe,
> Some unsuspected hoard of darling grief,
> Which they unseen may wail, and weep and mourn,
> And, glutton-like, alone devour

is not the thought of a shallow mind. It bears some sort of
kinship, however, to the extraordinary psychological perception which the poet, a mere boy, had shown in his study of
Heartwell, the old bachelor, in his first play. There seems no
sort of kinship between the thoughts of Almeria and the
seduction scene between Tattle and Miss Prue, in *Love for
Love*; but the instinctive regret that Congreve should have
been able to write that kind of thing as well as he did is an
irrational regret. We have seen the furies of fear and hate at
work in Lady Touchwood and Mellefont. Here is another
passage from the same play. Lady Froth has discovered that
Mr Brisk is in love with her:

Lady Froth. O be merry by all means.—Prince Volscius in love!
ha! ha! ha!
Brisk. O barbarous to turn me into ridicule! Yet, ha! ha! ha!—
the deuce take me, I can't help laughing myself, ha! ha! ha!—yet
by Heavens! I have a violent passion for your ladyship seriously.
Lady Froth. Seriously? Ha! ha! ha!
Brisk. Seriously, ha! ha! ha! Gad, I have for all I laugh.
Lady Froth. Ha! ha! ha!—What d'ye think I laugh at? Ha! ha!
ha!
Brisk. Me, egad, ha! ha!
Lady Froth. No, the deuce take me if I don't laugh at myself;
for hang me! if I have not a violent passion for Mr Brisk, ha! ha! ha!
Brisk. Seriously?
Lady Froth. Seriously, ha! ha! ha!
Brisk. That's well enough; let me perish, ha! ha! ha! O mira-
culous! what a happy discovery; ah, my dear charming Lady Froth!
Lady Froth. O my adored Mr Brisk!
[*They embrace.*]

Are they human? Not quite. We do but catch a glimpse of
them dancing their little formal piece of nonsense in a corner

William Congreve

of the stage during *The Good-Humoured Ladies*. But how delicious a caper it is! And how immeasurably far from the thick Jonsonian humours of Foresight the astrologer in *Love for Love* or of Wittol and Bluffe in *The Old Bachelor*!

Congreve could write excellently well in any style; and no matter what style he wrote in he showed the fineness, the aristocratic distinction (to use a current phrase) of his intellect; and sometimes with sudden audacity, as at the end of *The Old Bachelor*, and sometimes with very subtle adjustment, he could mingle his styles to make the whole that he wanted. With these powers and with that reputation Congreve must have needed a compelling reason to have left the theatre at the end of his seven wonderful years. And without likening him to Phœbus in the house of Admetus, one may justly ask whether he were not a little too fine a genius for his environment. The causes of the discord may have been two. The first is dangerous ground, from which all wise men keep until they are forced on to it: it is the relations of man and woman. Belinda in *The Old Bachelor* scarcely counts. She is a rudimentary Millamant, and her Bellmour is a coarse sketch for Mirabell. We come nearer in the Cynthia and Mellefont, whose love is put into *The Double-Dealer* as if they were only meant to set off the turbulent passions of Lady Touchwood and Maskwell and the butterfly dance of the Froths and Mr Brisk.

Mel. You're thoughtful, Cynthia?

Cyn. I'm thinking, though marriage makes man and wife one flesh, it leaves them still two fools: and they become more conspicuous by setting off one another.

Mel. That's only when two fools meet, and their follies are opposed.

Cyn. Nay, I have known two wits meet, and by the opposition of their wit render themselves as ridiculous as fools. 'Tis an odd game we're going to play at: what think you of drawing stakes and giving over in time?

The word 'game' gives uneasy Mellefont his lead, and he soon turns it all off into a jest. But not before we have caught a glimpse of a surprising thing: a woman who can talk straight and sensibly, and a woman who can be her lover's and her husband's friend, because she has a very sensitive respect for her own personality and for his. It was not a common idea in those days. And when it appeared full-grown in *The Way of the World* it may well have puzzled some and have offended others. One of the greatest services to the play rendered by its production at the Lyric Theatre, Hammersmith, was to show that Millamant and Mirabell (the Millamant of Miss Edith Evans, the Mirabell of Mr Robert Loraine) were not a pair of heartless flirts and their famous bargain the crackling of thorns under a pot. It would embolden the most timid to dare disagreement with Hazlitt and with George Meredith. Hazlitt thought Millamant 'nothing but a fine lady'. Meredith, with his head full of Célimène, thought her 'a type of the superior ladies who do not think'. What Congreve meant to show was a fine lady who could both think and love; and who respected herself and her lover too much to let marriage rob either of them of their true quality. 'Dwindle into a wife' indeed! Mirabell had better remember how she hated seeing him mixed up with the fools and gossips of the Cabal night; for she is even more eager than he that this 'odd game', as Cynthia called it, of living together shall be done without either party's dwindling. It is an idea of partnership and friendship which can still shock many women and scare most men; and it must be admitted that to entertain it as Congreve entertained it is at least to lay oneself open to dreams of a state of society and of human well-being very different from those commonly accepted by the cads and hussies who formed the greater part of the fine folk for whom he wrote. Now and then Congreve's very dialogue suggests that he felt his danger. In the last scene of *The Way of the World* we read:

Lady Wishfort. Well, Sir, take her, and with her all the joy I can give you.

Millamant. Why does not the man take me? Would you have me give myself to you over again?

Mirabell. Ay, and over and over again. [*Kisses her hand.*]

It is perfect. There is nothing more gallant, gracious, tender and (as Johnson would say) natural in all English drama. But

Mirabell did not stop there. This was, after all, the theatre, and 'the proud usurpers of the pit' must not be puzzled or bored. And so, with one of his inimitably deft little twists of tone, Congreve lets it all slip down again to the usual 'Restoration comedy' level of the flesh, and in bursts Sir Wilfull Witwoud with a hint of bawdry and a call for a dance.

'He was always seeking the finest quality in everything, in life as well as in writing.' He was 'hungry for beauty'. He had 'a longing to find the world finer than it really is, a poetic fastidiousness and a depth of feeling'. The more one reads Congreve the truer does Mr Dobrée's estimate of him declare itself. When he wrote *The Way of the World* he achieved a beauty which English comedy had never achieved before and has never equalled. Yet *The Way of the World* has not the faultless self-sufficiency of *The School for Scandal*. The form has never before been refined into poetry so exquisite; but the poet shows some hesitancy, even some little insincerity, in entrusting his most cherished ideas, the ideas that he most wanted to express, to a form which he knew to be still conditioned by dependence on the public intelligence. The form proved too fine for the town; the ideas too new. The town rejected the best he had given it. Not only that, he was left with the uneasy feeling that it was not the best that he could give it, with the regret that he had stooped even so far as he did to conciliate the vulgar, and with the conviction that to try again would only be again to expose his nearest and dearest thoughts and dreams to Petulants and Witwouds, Tattles and Brisks. His feet were winged, but he must wear the bandages of the gouty. His eyes saw strange beauties deep hidden under human affectations; but he must pull his hat over his brows and keep his vision and his thoughts to himself.

J. M. BARRIE AS DRAMATIST
(1942)

No reader of Professor Dover Wilson's *What Happens in 'Hamlet'* but must wish that the practice of printing plays had not led on inevitably to the practice of reading plays and to the still sadder practice of thinking about plays. Shakespeare —for the most part a single-minded man—took full advantage of the ephemeral nature of the acted drama. To any single scene the audience is bound to play Bernardo, Horatio, and Marcellus to the Ghost—''Tis here! 'Tis here! 'Tis gone'; or, in more modern terms, 'That's the Ghost, that was!' There is no looking before and after, turning back a few pages to find a discrepancy or forward to see whether the author will remember what he has shown or told us. The coherence and the singleness of more than one play by Shakespeare depend on his ability to prevent our thinking it over while we are looking and listening.

That being so with Shakespeare, how should it not be much more so with Barrie, who was no single-minded man, who lived, indeed, constantly in one or other of at least two worlds, and whose mission as dramatist was to bring them both, or all, together without our catching him at it? The publication of this new definitive edition of his plays[1] gives a good opportunity of seeing how impossible it is, printed play in hand, not to catch him at it, and not to be lured from the enjoyment of his dramatic genius and art into gropings after the secrets of his private mind. Mr A. E. Wilson has left out no piece by Barrie which can help to the understanding and enjoyment of his drama. Mature playgoers may wish that they could freshen their memories of some few—*La Politesse*, for instance,

[1] *The Plays of J. M. Barrie.* Edited by A. E. Wilson. Hodder and Stoughton.

and *Josephine*, and *Punch*, and even *Rosy Rapture*; and in the very act of wishing may bless Mr Wilson for saving them from almost certain disappointment. But he starts with *Walker, London*; he gives *The Wedding Guest* as well as *The Professor's Love Story* and *The Little Minister*, and he stoops even to *Little Mary* and *Old Friends*. He has left out nothing, that is, that can help the reader to watch the advance of Barrie the craftsman, the playwright, as well as the very irregular development of Barrie the dramatist from the story of Gavin Dishart to the story of David.

The skill of the craftsman is plain already in *Walker, London*: the sub-human trivialities of the farce are so trickily handled as to prove that, if Barrie had not been bothered with a mystical mind and a diffident temper and a ruthless ambition, he could have been the greatest writer of 'well made' plays ever known. From the very first, he could think his stories in terms of the theatre; and without assiduous cultivation of that gift he would never have accomplished certain master-pieces of theatrical effect—the cooking-pot at the end of Act II of *Crichton* and the boom of the gun during the dance in Act III (those were Walkley's selections for first prize), the opening scenes of *What Every Woman Knows* and of *Dear Brutus*, hard to equal for rousing curiosity, the disappear-ance of Mary Rose on the island in the second Act, and (perhaps most skilful of all) the first entrance—'Mother, I have killed a lion!'—of the Boy David. Much more than craftsmanship went to the making of that last effect, and, indeed, of some of the others; but only a consummately 'theatre-minded' master of his medium could have brought them off.

He loved the very difficulties and absurdities resulting from the physical and the formal elements in that medium, from the tell-tale 'click' of the act-drop to the airs and graces of the actress (is there anywhere a shrewder or a more heart-winning description of Ellen Terry than in *Rosalind*, especially in the long stage-direction about 'Beatrice Page's famous bag'?). 'Everything may be real on the stage except the books', he remarks with no shadow of provocation in a stage-direction to *A Kiss for Cinderella*; and even in *Alice Sit-by-the-Fire* there are two little surviving occasions for a smile—the screen behind which the stage-struck young women 'mechanically as it were, pop' at a chance of eavesdropping, and the gentle-man's gentleman who, before the curtain rises on his master's chambers at midnight, may be conceived trying the lamp, which is to be knocked over, and making sure the lady will not stick in the door, through which she is to escape unobserved. His pleasure in that sort of thing helped him in small matters of construction. Which of his incidental pieces was it that began with Miss Hilda Trevelyan and a telephone performing the functions of Sir Walter Ralegh and Sir Christopher Hatton in *The Critic*? His pleasure in that sort of thing helped him in greater matters. For good or ill, it suggested the visions in the last Act of *The Boy David*, the constructing of which he —an amateur, after all, at staging—had to leave to professional skill.

Barrie's love of theatrical detail and process was rather like Kipling's love of tools and ships and motor-cars and machinery. This boyishness in Kipling led him on to venerate good crafts-manship and to abhor slick and sloppy work. How far, if at all, it tied him down or blinded him to other things that make up human life is not our concern here. Barrie's boyishness, his love of playing with the theatre, is, perhaps, the cardinal fact. Here was a world that he could play with, a world that looked as if it was ready to acknowledge him as its master and to obey his orders. How large and exciting and infinitely various a toy for a boy to play with! A live dog, with a will of its own, or a mechanical railway, which depends upon rails, could never be either so obedient or so constantly new. It was a thousand pities that he could not play with the theatre without having to grapple with what the theatre is there to reflect, or ex-pound, or, in its own way, to play with—obstinate stuff called reality, which often refuses to obey and sometimes makes the playing boy look rather silly. On the first production of *The Admirable Crichton* (it was forty years ago next

November, but Barrie was already a man of over forty), Walkley wrote:

> Mr Barrie not only has ideas, but he can *play* with them. Never, we surmise, has this philosophy of the 'return to nature' been so pleasantly, so fancifully, so frolicsomely expounded.

Among the ideas which Barrie had and succeeded in playing with, a few are fixed ideas, instructive, no doubt, in the study of his make-up, but merely obedient and useful in his drama. There is the brave woman idea (Moira Loney, Maggie Wylie, Cinderella, Mrs Dowey and many another), though, indeed, this is involved in an almost Strindbergian mixture of morbid adoration and morbid fear of women. There is the father-and-son awkwardness (in *Alice Sit-by-the-Fire, Little Mary, The New World, A Well-Remembered Voice*). There is baby-worship, *passim*. With those three ideas Barrie could play as he pleased. He liked to see himself playing with ideas, even to show himself playing with ideas. He is Lob, little Lob, the master of the house, in *Dear Brutus*, and Sam Smith, little old Sam Smith, the master of the house, in *Shall We Join the Ladies?* And he is Peter Pan, little Peter Pan, the master in the Never Land and in the Tree-Tops. And nearly always, as Walkley said, he plays with his ideas pleasantly, fancifully, frolicsomely. If only we could see and hear each play while it is being acted before us, and never remember a word nor a sight in any one of them, how masterfully, eternally, incomparably charming would be the drama of J. M. Barrie!

But the very feeblest memory must retain some of those momentarily enchanting words and movements; and nearly all his plays are printed in this and other books, and we poor human beings look before and after and pine for an innocence that is not. A worse trouble is that Barrie himself knew that reality was not, like the theatre, a pretty toy for a child to play with. Child-worship is a very different matter from baby-worship; and, if your ideal life is the child-life and your perfect wisdom the intuitive wisdom of childhood, ideas are likely to resent being played with, as islands may resent being visited.

Barrie, it has been said, was too much diverted from the substance of a play to the manner. He would play with an idea; and, when he had done playing, it would suddenly be seen in its proper nature, like a snake-charmer's snake with its fangs undrawn, and the snake-charmer's face twisted in a mocking grin. Dear little Lob with his flowers and his pretty ways—what is he (when the play is over and we are out in the dark again) but a cruel little fiend, luring poor fools on to see themselves as they are and as they are doomed to go on being? What happens in the end to that idea of the return to nature which has been so pleasantly, so fancifully, so frolic-somely expounded? We may smile at the solemn critic who recently asked what chance there was for democracy and so forth on that unhappy island 'where women appear to enjoy their own subservience'. It sounds comic; but perhaps it is serio-comic. The whole pretty thing breaks in pieces when nature falls on its knees before convention, and strength out of its noble obligation to weakness, commits suicide, and a woman denies her love. Little Sam Smith, who entertains at dinner all the possible murderers of his brother, may sit 'beaming on his guests, like an elderly cupid'; if he did not gloat over torturing his victims, he would have 'called in the Yard' like any other decent fellow in a murder yarn. We know, too, what happened to Peter Pan when the world refused to go on being his toy. 'If he could get the hang of the thing right'—but he cannot. He can only 'shrink up from existence', forget the lost boys, forget Jas Hook, forget Tinker Bell, forget even Wendy, and be alone with himself.

All this is mighty solemn. There would be no need for a word of it if plays only existed while they were being performed. But the printed book whips up the trouble begun by memory and thought. It shows that Barrie himself was bothered by the stubbornness of ideas that declined to wear the pretty clothes he arranged upon their ungainly or repulsive forms, putting, as someone phrased it, a wreath of roses ('such a pretty wreath!' as Barrie would have said) on a skull. He was sometimes in two minds himself whether the pretty clothes or the idea were what he really wanted to show us.

In *A Kiss for Cinderella* it is a matter rather of taste than of idea. (In parenthesis, it is only in this play that a serious misprint has caught our eyes. Little discrepancies between names in the Dramatis Personae and in the text are easily excused in such a collected edition as this; but 'infallayble'— three times on one page—cannot possibly spell the Policeman's famous 'infall*i*able'.) The difficulty comes at the end. Memory, contemporary Press notices and Mr Denis Mackail's *The Story of J. M. B.* combine to record that in performance the play had a 'happy ending', that what Mr Mackail well calls 'the longed-for and essential kiss' meant that Cinderella would get well and marry the Policeman. That was what roused a critic of a recent revival to wish that Barrie could have made up his mind whether the girl was twenty years old or ten, mother or baby, fairy or flesh-and-blood. In print, the play does not end happily: Cinderella is not to get well. And the Policeman knows it, for 'Dr Bodie has told him something'; and he does not so much kiss her as 'press her face to him, so that he may not see its transparency'.

The difference is just the difference between smiles and tears, between gladness and a heart-ache—no great matter, perhaps, for serious and practical people to worry about when the lovers are both creatures of playful, unworldly fantasy. True, one must be hopelessly serious and practical not to feel that it matters intensely whether the pair, even in the book and much, much more on the stage in human form, are to be happy or not. But it is not a difficulty of the utmost urgency and moment to all serious and practical people like the end of *Dear Brutus*. Here Barrie did the opposite of what he had done in *A Kiss for Cinderella*. The question is: can any of us take advantage of a second chance, or are we all doomed to follow to the end that wrong turning? Does Lob's experiment ever have any permanent effect? One of the subjects of it asks the question of the man most likely to know; and his answer is: 'So far as I know, not often, miss; but, I believe, once in a while.' And a stage-direction follows:

There is hope in this for the brave ones. If we could wait long enough we might see the Dearths breasting their way into the light.

Stage-directions are not read out in the theatre. What the theatre has told us and shown us in word and in action is that Dearth's entrancing friend and daughter was only a dream, and that when he found that out his hand immediately began to shake again and the watery eye of the drunkard came back. If Barrie had had anything near to a conviction that reformation was not denied us, that even only once in a while a second chance could be taken and held, he would have made that faith clear through some stronger evidence than Dearth's sporting word of gratitude to Lob for the hour of delusive happiness. In the event he hedges. He leaves us, in the book, compelled to conclude (and how one hates having to find fault with Lob, or with Peter!) that he funked at the last minute. He had been so busy with the manner of his play that he was diverted from the substance. It was not till he had got the rose-wreath in place that he saw how hideous was the grimace of the grinning skull. He had been playing pleasantly, fancifully, frolicsomely, with humanity's despair.

That, as we see his drama in its successive growth, was the last time that he was afraid. He could never give up playing; and all that is so ingeniously and so inimitably his own in fancy and frolic was not his to use or throw away at will. It was his essential medium of expression. But between the way he uses it in *Dear Brutus* and the way he uses it in *Mary Rose* there is the difference between running away from reality and proclaiming that fancy and frolic could be as real as terrible matter-of-fact. Barrie's mastery of dramatic art was once, but only once, more finely revealed than in the matter, as well as the manner, of the disappearance of Mary Rose. He is no longer afraid to say that life can be dreadful. With true artistic instinct, he chose a supernatural agency—in itself, no doubt, neither good nor evil—for the ruin of one innocent and lovely life, and the infliction on other lives of much undeserved misery and fear. From *Thomas of Erceldoune* and other old legends he drew magical beauty; and the more beautiful he made the strangeness, the more horrible became the suffering from which not even death could set the unoffending victim free.

Mary Rose, very probably, was a projection of Barrie; the island was the life of play; the plain world of the manor-house and of marriage (we have to allow the author his indispensable measure of baby-worship) is obstinate reality. But that is by the way. In *Mary Rose* for the first time Barrie is brave enough to be honest. Reality can be horrible; but it shall not be pushed out of the way, as it had been when he concocted the artful sugar-cakes of *The Professor's Love Story* and *The Little Minister*, nor shall there be any pretence that the rose-wreath is adorning a head with life and hope in it. At last he has looked straight at reality and learned that he can make beauty of it—a heart-breaking beauty more poignant and more purifying than any of his renowned 'pathos'.

There was one more step forward to take; and he took it. He wrote *The Boy David*. What Mr Granville-Barker has written about that play in his introduction to the separate edition of it (Peter Davies, 1938) will have comforted and enlightened a great many admirers of Barrie, who doubted whether he could have been such a fool as report declared to challenge the Bible story, or his play such a dismal mock-fantasy as it was made out to be. Barrie's chivalrous patience during the years between the writing of the play and its production makes one of the most grateful passages in Mr Mackail's biography; and there can be no harm in thinking that he was the less worried by the delay and damped by the disappointment because he knew that this was a work of genius that could afford to be heedless of the present.

All his life he had been inspired—inspired with magic and mystery that may have been as much national as personal, and with a (truly poetical) power of association that was all his own and not to be compassed by taking thought. A higher kind of inspiration fills *The Boy David* with unearthly beauty. At the very end of his career he found out what it was that he had been groping after in Peter Pan. It was not the domination of reality by play; the making the world his toy, to be treated with kindly contempt, as by Peter, or cruelly, as by Lob, but always to be dominated. 'Wendy, I've killed a pirate!' cries the boy Michael. 'Mother, I have killed a lion!' cries the Boy David. They are both children; but one is childishness as distinct from manhood, the other is the childhood at the core of all humanity:

> Other One, David is in darkness. Will you not tell me what to do? (*Appealing*) Other One?

He goes off with his toys—his sling and his harp. He is still a child, and on occasion as boastful as ever was Peter Pan with his cockcrow. But here is 'the intuitive wisdom of childlike humanity' aware of that Other One; and towards that integration of God and man Barrie, we may believe, had been groping all his life. The technical faults in the play are pretty clear to all; the technical beauties of it will be clearer still to those who read Mr Granville-Barker. Time and thought, we believe, will exalt this play to its proper place as the supreme achievement of Barrie's genius.

CHRISTMAS REFLECTIONS

THE GOOD LIFE—THOUGHTS
FOR CHRISTMAS

(1939)

This time last year the threat of war had been so lately lifted that, as Mr Middleton Murry put it in this *Supplement*, there was something pretty miraculous for most of us in the mere absence of war; 'this simple negative boon shines to us with the brightness of a gift new dropped from Heaven: as indeed it is'. In Bethlehem, birthplace of the Prince of Peace, there was no peace. In China and in Spain there was war. In Central Europe the powers of evil, half in secret, half in defiance, were creeping forward along the road which, hope and trust though we might, we knew in our heart of hearts must bring them where only at the price of our shame could we tolerate them. Yet we did well to make the most and the best of that peace which was no peace but only an absence of war in our own and certain other countries. So far as it went, it was a positive good. Since it had been won for us by our own Prime Minister at the eleventh hour, it lent a missionary fervour to our prayers for the peace of the rest of the world; and we could go ahead with our preparations for a 'Merry Christmas' with ardent gratitude for our good fortune.

We were not exactly in a false position, but our merriment was poised on a very narrow base if our own immunity from war were all. Bereft of that excuse for merriment, we ought, on that showing, to turn away our eyes from the coming Christmas, merely to save ourselves the agonizing contrast between the promise of the angelic host and the performance of the human hosts. If happiness depends upon peace, what happiness can be sought in a Christmas—possibly only the first of several Christmases—during the most frightful war ever known? In the minds of those who are old enough a phrase here and there from the last war—'But I was thinking of the young men'—or a memory—Drury Lane Theatre packed with elementary school children singing, not idly, but in the hushed and earnest voice of prayer, 'Keep the home fires burning'—such memories can now again wring the heart with the pity of it, and make last Christmas's mere absence of war seem the highest of blessings. To pretend that it is not so or to harden the heart against it is to be a traitor to oneself. To let the pity of it black out all the light of happiness, of Christmas merriment, is to be a traitor to oneself and to England, and more than England as well.

If what they tell us and counsel us is true, we of the Home Front are in a more honourable state than ever before. In the Napoleonic wars life, we know, at home went on very much as usual. Jane Austen had brothers in the Navy; but her world was so little affected by the wars that the Navy might have existed only to give William Price a profession and enable Admiral Croft to rent Kellynch Hall. There was the threat of invasion, it is true—and *The Trumpet Major* and the scenes on Rainbarrows' Beacon in *The Dynasts* give the measure of its weight upon the public mind. Statesmen, no doubt, knew hours of deep anxiety, and shared them with those in their confidence; but the nation in general knew nothing of such hazard as we stand in to-day. It was easy enough to bear up and be cheerful under such conditions, especially as men's minds were not troubled in those days by any doubts about the nation's right to defend itself with the bodies and lives of the flower of its manhood.

Now for the first time (if the fate of Poland is any guide, and if what they tell us is true) the non-combatant is entitled to feel that at least he is not sending young men to mutilation, agony and death at no cost to himself except a little easily borne privation. Exposed to dangers unimaginable by the home-keeping English of King George III's days, he has now an almost equal right with the fighting-men to snatch at every moment of respite, to enjoy every good thing within his scope, to make merry at Christmas and at every other opportunity that offers. And warriors and civilians alike have better right and reason to rejoice than they had a year ago. We are not now uneasily watching the movements of the evil beast which we were ostensibly committed to considering harmless, knowing full well in the marrow of our bones that it can never be trusted. We need no longer wheedle and humour it, nor pretend that foul offences against God and man committed within its own territory are no concern of ours. We are at open war with it, pledged to fight it to the death; and the new candour lifts a load from our conscience that was heavier than all the loads that warfare lays upon our nerves and spirits.

A mind turned on Christmas is inevitably a mind turned on the Christmas message. Next Christmas it will only be natural to lean towards the Vulgate version of it: *Pax hominibus bonae voluntatis*; peace to men of good will, and no peace to men of evil will, breakers of faith, corrupters of youth, torturers of the body and enslavers of the soul. But at present our concern is with a humbler matter—with our proper attitude to the familiar Christmas merriment, and to all the good things and pleasant things and lovely things in common life. When a love-affair gone wrong or some other heavy blow knocks him out, a young man is prone to take all beauty and happiness as an insult to himself. What right have roses to bloom or children to laugh when he himself is all pain and sorrow? So it is, to some degree, with less personal griefs and older sufferers. The nations are all pain and sorrow, and their pain and sorrow pierce to the inmost privacies of the family. It is unpardonable heartlessness, some think, to show any sign of relaxation and enjoyment. Nothing for it but to go grimly through the bad time, doggedly declining all solace until evil has been conquered.

That may be a good way, but it is not the best way. We have to ask ourselves whether, on that principle, the pain and sorrow in the world are not at every moment of time too great to allow of any one's being happy. And out of that arises the further question whether even such an increase of pain and sorrow as these last few years have seen has in any degree diminished the positive available amount of pleasure and happiness. Bob Cratchit's Christmas goose was, after all, a very good goose, although it was not a turkey; and that homely and seasonable illustration may suggest that the Cratchit spirit of thankful enjoyment is no bad example. Good and evil are not mutually exclusive. No matter how huge the bulk of the world's misery, the sources of happiness and (let us not be afraid of the word) of pleasure are none the fewer for it. From too many of the men, women and children in Europe and Asia those sources have been snatched by violence; they will never make merry again until we restore to them a life fit for human beings. But with ourselves it is not so, yet. Our compassion for the sufferers will be none the more pitiful, our labours to rescue them will be none the wiser or the more devoted, if we shut our eyes to all that still may make our own lives pleasant.

On condition of doing our utmost to save others from misery we may claim a right to take all the happiness we may find in our own course. We may venture further and see it as sound policy; and, perhaps, without extravagance, be permitted to call it a duty. We are fighting to destroy a form of tyranny which, setting aside its positive cruelties, degrades the idea of human nature and of human life. Under it the human being ceases to be a live organism with an independent being of its own and dwindles into a cog in a machine; and human life is robbed of all amenity, all individuality, all power of self-expression. If we are fighting to put a better life in place of this degraded life we should surely be at the same time living to the same end. We should be asserting in our own lives the superiority of what we regard as the good life for civilized human beings.

We need not be afraid of overdoing it. Not among our youth only there will be foolish people taking advantage of unusual conditions to indulge themselves and others in the wrong, the destructive kinds of pleasure; and, as in the last War, those who know better will be only half-hearted in their attempts to check the folly, especially in the young. Let *them* eat and drink, for to-morrow they die! But for the rest, for those with no taste for dissipation, whose pleasure lies in things at once simpler and subtler, before we are through with this mighty undertaking, circumstance will see to it that we are none too rich in temptations to go soft. Yet to deny ourselves for any motive except the increase of our strength would be a form of treachery to our own ideal of the good life. Cheerfulness to order, a show of heartiness at the bidding of a Government poster, is a form of pretence which the cold wind of fact is likely soon to blow out of being. But the positive good remains, for each man to cultivate in his double capacity as exponent of the good life and the guardian of his own free spirit.

There we come upon another pretext for seeing this alertness to the positive good as a duty. The higher that human nature ascends above its primitive fears and shames, the better it knows how true enjoyment feeds and fortifies the spirit. Hedonism is spiritual death. By shutting out all that it finds ugly and painful, it loses touch with reality, and reduces the art of living to a device for running away from life. But to look fair and square at evil, to recognize its existence not as a fact merely but as a challenge, is the only way to find the true good in the things that please. They become then our sources of strength in the conduct of the life that we believe to be good and our defence against the life that we know to be evil.

In this process of becoming which we call life, it is useless to play for certainty or finality. We need not bother about the perfectibility of man, as idealists were wont to under the spell of the French Revolution. But we may fairly see two kinds of life pulling in opposite directions—the evil life that goes by ill will, hatred, greed, cruelty, the oppression of man, and the good life that goes by good will. Till lately it had seemed as if the life of good will was gaining pretty rapidly in strength over the life of ill will; and it was possible to do something more than play with the idea of humanity outgrowing old hatred, suspicion, and fear, and turning consciously and deliberately to the ways of sympathy and brotherly love. There has been a bad setback in that progress. The good life and the evil life are at grips. Yet even should the worst happen and the good life go down before the evil life so that there was no more power of living it in this country than there is in Poland or in German and Austrian Jewry, the truth and the virtue of it would remain the same. It is the good life because its motive is the grateful enjoyment of all that is lovable in humanity, in art, in nature, in thought or in sense. It would increase and refine the quantity and quality of life, not thwart, enslave and debase it. It insists upon the individual freedom of the spirit and the liberty to grow without being stunted and cramped into a mould. It must needs enjoy, and in enjoying create, beauty of whatever kind. It is an affirmation set up against a base denial.

OF IVORY TOWERS
(1940)

Research, conducted under difficulties, has not yet revealed to this present, and ignorant, writer who first used the phrase 'ivory tower' as a term of contempt, nor why it is that other writers have suddenly caught it up, so that in book and in newspaper it has become a commonplace. Mr Aldous Huxley is not one to slip into clichés; yet his new little book, *Vulgarity in Literature*, has its ivory towers: 'When we venture out of our ivory towers', we are instantly swallowed by 'a queer, rather sinister and finally quite incomprehensible monster', called Nature.

We are to understand that every man has an ivory tower like a Norman keep, or one of the towers at San Gimignano; built to keep enemies out, and perhaps with inadequate recognition of its power to keep the owner in, even against his will. The ivory tower is a makeshift for the Freudian womb, towards which, in Mr Huxley's words, we are always nostalgically yearning. It is said to be of ivory, no doubt because ivory is costly and beautiful but a flimsy material for building; and the implication is that something much tougher and less alluring would do better for a structure that is designed to warn off the outer world and to delight its owner alone with its inner beauty. And whatever the reason for building it high, for making it a tower, it is not that its owner and his friends may go up to the top and admire the view of the world outside or of the heavens above. The first postulate is that it shall be self-contained and self-sufficient in order that the outer world, above it or below, may be regarded as having ceased to exist.

All who scoff at ivory towers are agreed that the object of

them is to provide each owner with an escape from so much of the life outside as does not please him. They take for granted that, in escaping thus, he leaves behind him something known as 'reality' and shuts himself up with a figment. There seems to be no end to the variety of possible figments. Hundreds of thousands of people escape happily into the life exhibited by Hollywood films. Such an escape rouses as much scorn in the bosoms of certain others as does the escape into a cheery Browningesque confidence in a future life where all will get compensation for their sufferings in this life. Some see all art as so many ivory towers; some, pure mathematics or metaphysics; some, carnal self-indulgence. In the infinity of disagreement, one belief is common to all—that all within an ivory tower is a denial or distortion of reality and truth. What is reality, what is truth? We stay in vain for an answer.

The oldest and most general conflict, perhaps, is between 'realism' and 'romanticism'. To Ford Madox Ford, for instance, romanticism was an escape from truth into falsehood. The subtler mind of Mr Aldous Huxley turns the object into a different light. To him the universality which the classicists (Racine, for instance) gave to human nature by abstracting the corporeal element of the passions reduced man to an algebraical symbol. For himself, he has 'a taste for the lively, the mixed and the incomplete in art, preferring it to the universal and the chemically pure'; and we must leave it to him to decide just where—since a writer such as he is cannot help imposing a pattern on life which is not to be found in his subject-matter —he will draw the line between the classical-universal and literature which shall 'render adequately that infinitely complex and mysterious thing, actual reality'. Actual reality lies, we observe, outside the ivory tower of the classicists. But what of Mr Charles Morgan, an author commonly supposed to live in a very remote and very lofty tower built of the very smoothest ivory? The review in *The Times* of Mr Morgan's latest novel, *The Voyage*, admits, indeed, that the book is one of those that delivers the reader 'from the oppression of an outward reality that has turned evil', but it delivers him by guiding him to 'a deeper level of the spirit'—where, presumably, truth and reality are stronger and purer than on the levels nearer the surface. And here is another light on reality. In a new book (of which more later) Professor G. H. Hardy, the mathematician, observes in a footnote: 'Many people, of course, use "sentimentalism" as a term of abuse for other people's decent feelings, and "realism" as a disguise for their own brutality.'

The sort of people who take refuge from real life in Hollywood films, or jazz music, or alcohol, are too inarticulate to defend their choice. In their behalf it might be suggested that it is impossible to get away from reality, and that there must be some measure of reality even in a Royal Academy historical picture, a crooner's song, or the legendary exploits of an ancient Celtic hero. When their means of escape were sneered at, they would understand no more than that the realists wanted to maintain that nothing could be real unless it was unpleasant, whereas their own innocent trust in experience persuaded them that a happy love-story, a good song or a pot of beer were every bit as real as a skin disease, or the sinking of the children's ship, or the mind of Herr Himmler. Stronger minds can face the accuser, and declare that a state of mind is not proved to be humbug merely by calling it an ivory tower, or some other nickname, and that for their part they have chosen what the scoffer calls an ivory tower to be their home precisely because they find reality within it and unreality, or less pure reality outside it.

To return to Mr Hardy's little book, *A Mathematician's Apology*—the author is a 'real mathematician', which means, in the clumsy popular usage so different from his own subtle precision, a 'pure mathematician'. He recognizes two sorts of reality. There is physical reality, the reality of 'the material world, the world of day and night, earthquakes and eclipses, the world which physical science tries to describe'. There is also mathematical reality. And to Mr Hardy (though not, he warns us, to all 'real' mathematicians) that reality is—once more to be abrupt and clumsy—more real than physical reality.

I believe that mathematical reality lies outside us, that our function is to discover or *observe* it, and that the theorems which we prove, and which we describe grandiloquently as our 'creations', are simply our notes of our observations.

And a little later he writes:

Pure mathematics...seems to me a rock on which all idealism founders; 317 is a prime, not because we think so, or because our minds are shaped in one way rather than another, but *because it is so*, because mathematical reality is built that way.

Mr Aldous Huxley's reality lies in the particular and the temporary; Mr Hardy's is first cousin of the universal—of (let us whisper it) the Absolute. And he is prepared to defend the employment of it as a mere ivory tower, a mere means of escape from the world which to him is less real, to most people more real.

When the world is mad, a mathematician may find in mathematics an incomparable anodyne. For mathematics is, of all the arts and sciences, the most austere and the most remote, and a mathematician should be of all men the one who can most easily take refuge where, as Bertrand Russell says, 'One at least of our nobler impulses can best escape from the dreary exile of the actual world.'

Mr Hardy has more than that to say about escaping into this remote refuge; but, before we come to it, we may turn from one who insists that 'real mathematics must be justified as art if it can be justified at all' to one whose ivory tower is art in the more usual sense. If any reader of Mr Aldous Huxley's vicious sentence about 'neo-ninetyites who...play kittenishly around with their wax flowers and stuffed owls and Early Victorian beadwork' should catch himself thinking of Mr Sacheverell Sitwell's *Sacred and Profane Love*, wherein an ivory tower is exquisitely furnished and very choicely adorned, let him do penance for a natural but reprehensible slip. Mr Sitwell is another who defends his own escape on the ground that within his ivory tower there is more reality, more truth, than there is outside it. A chapter in that book proclaims the right and the duty of the artist to create his own world and to live in it. If, as artist, he condescends to less complete forms of reality, he will have been the architect of his own decline.

To say, as has been said lately by a popular poet, that no author can hope to write a good book unless he joins the working-class movement is as grotesque an absurdity as any utterance of the mid-Victorians. The workers only despise such sentimental affiliation.... Until they are educated, and unless they are, it will be one worker in a million who wants to read a modern poem. To deny this is to be sentimental in just the manner that Holman Hunt was sentimental when he said that it made him frightened to draw a wild flower. The artist must not throw away his prerogative so cheaply.

There are, then, men ready to vow that their remote and sparsely populated spiritual homes hold more reality than the worlds of the realists. Perhaps it would not matter very much in ordinary times. But when in a harsh world we are all drawing our breath in pain, when our form of civilization is threatened with death and can hope for nothing better than to be half-killed in killing its enemy, the little pigs that build their houses of bricks have a right to ask the piglings that build in straw and in twigs what they are going to do about it. Even grant that they were right in seeing the truest truth, the most real reality inside their houses of straw and of twigs, their ivory towers, it seems obvious that, if they run for refuge to them now, they are not neutral, but allies of the big bad wolf, just as the absolute pacifists are the most devout servants of brute force. We must all be practical; we must all be of some use. Of what use are these escapists? Mr Hardy makes no bones about it:

A science or an art may be said to be 'useful' if its development increases, even indirectly, the material well-being and comfort of men, if it promotes happiness, using that word in a crude and commonplace way.

The kinds of mathematics that are useful in that sense do not include his own real mathematics, and he is not at all sure, considering their use in warfare, that they have not done more harm to man than good. But 'real mathematics', he writes proudly, 'has no effects on war'. Real mathematics is of no use in the sense which Mr Hardy ascribes to the word. But not on that account must it be condemned as of no (shall we say?) service to mankind. Mr Hardy himself will go no farther than this—that he has added something to knowledge, and helped others to add more, and that

these somethings have a value which differs in degree only, and not in kind, from that of the creations of the great mathematicians, or of any of the other artists, great or small, who have left some kind of memorial behind them.

Mr Sitwell comes a little closer than that to the artist's responsibility to society: 'It is only by spiritual or imaginative increase that the world can be saved'; and it is his part as writer (that is to say, as artist) to help make that increase. Of its immediate effect he takes little heed. 'Our aim, therefore', he writes, 'is neither a religious nor a moral lesson' (still less a political or an economic lesson) 'but an experience of a work of art. If this appeals only to a few persons, so much the better. It will not die so quickly'—wherein speaks not the arrogance of the artist, but his faith.

You cannot make people good, it has been said in our own day, except by Act of Parliament; and thus does totalitarianism insinuate the thin end of its wedge into our democratic society. From every ivory tower comes the answer that within the little world of man there are regions where Acts of Parliament mean nothing, and that these regions hold no less reality— that some of them hold much more reality—than those claimed by the realists. The disaster threatening our form of civilization is more than a material, a political, an economic disaster; and activities that are every bit as 'useless' in that sense as Mr Hardy's real mathematics and Mr Sitwell's experience of a work of art are needed to protect it. To sur- render these activities to the urgency of practical needs would be to shorten the stature of the human soul. And perhaps the realists, the scoffers at ivory towers, are prone to forget one very obvious fact—that the most fastidious escapist cannot shut all his faculties up within his ivory tower for every moment of every day and night. In his spare time, so to speak, he might be found in the ranks, at sea, in the air, or in an ambulance squad, patrolling his beat, sitting on committees. Indeed, he is likely to do all the better work on those levels for the spirit which buoys his soul above them.

THE AGE OF GOLD

(1941)

A brave article on the future of Norway, published in *The Times* of 14 November, contained this sentence: 'We have our fisheries and timber industries; we have also enormous quantities of unused water power.' To the heart of one admiring reader, the second clause struck chill. Fisheries and timber industries chimed with his idea of Norway; a country meet to be inhabited by the 'small and hardy fishing and agricultural population' which Maurice Hewlett foresaw for a free and happy England. Unused water power brought in the notion of machinery; and hotfoot after machinery came the industrial era, the mechanization of human life, the frenzy of commercial rivalry and the artificial economic barriers to international good will.

The repugnance and its associations were purely sentimental and unfair. For one thing, neither fishing nor forestry can be carried on nowadays without machinery; for another thing, our sentimental reader had in other days and far distant countries been exalted, not depressed, by the man-made lakes among the mountain heights, the terrific fall of the penstock, and at the foot the power-house, with machines in it that seemed to think. In *Paul et Virginie* Paul makes water run as he, not as Nature, wills; and we feel that it is very clever and charming of him. To accept in eighteenth-century Mauritius on a one-man, idyllic scale what we deprecate in twentieth-century Norway on a great and industrial scale is like being shocked at, say, Armour's in Chicago, which does with the utmost efficiency and in huge quantites what is being less well done in small quantites by slaughter-houses that our sensibility overlooks. Once the thought of the power-house was allowed to lead to the thought of the factories that it served, it had lost its charm. To the machines, there and in the factories, sentiment attributed the faults in our working of the industrial system. Searching for some reason for his sudden sentimental caprice, the puzzled reader began to wonder how much of it was due to the poets, and especially to those scrappily remembered from a far-off classical education.

Redeunt Saturnia regna is a tag that wakes echoes; the 'age of gold' rouses the 'bronze age' and the 'iron age'—phrases which oddly bring with them a connotation of the periods of modern anthropological science. In Hesiod's cycle the bronze age was the third, an age of terrible fighters and murderers; but the fifth, the iron age, that in which man was then living, was worse, an age of unnatural strife, father against child, guest against host, friend against friend. Are we still in the iron age, or have we passed into a sixth and even worse? Accounts vary; but all are agreed that there once was, while Saturn or Kronos ruled in heaven, an age of gold. In that age gold was perhaps the substance of which man was made, but was certainly not either used in work or desired as a possession or a means of exchange. The *auri sacra fames* was the death of the age of gold. Not the substance but its misuse did the mischief.

And it was the encroachment into human life of ever less worthy metals—gold, silver, bronze, iron—which 'brought death into the world, and all our woe'. What, we ask, could the Greeks and Romans, with their Heath Robinson ideas of machinery, their celestial blacksmiths, their elementary swords and spears, their conception of a shield, for Achilles or for Aeneas, as a fine chance for aesthetic display— what could they know of the horrors of which metal and machinery are capable? Deep in man's being there must lurk a primitive fear and hatred of metal, which not all his acquired passion for machinery can root out. Kipling's own McAndrew must have harboured it, all unknown to himself, somewhere.

All the poetic authorities agree that once there was a Saturnian era, an age of gold, an unmetalled age, in which

life was pure, simple and happy, and Nature needed no compulsion to bring forth her gifts in due season.

> Cum domitis nemo Cererem jactaret in arvis,
> Venturisque malas prohiberet fructibus herbas,
> Annua sed saturae complerent horrea messes,
> Ipse suo flueret Bacchus pede, mellaque lentis
> Penderent foliis, et pinguis Pallas olivae
> Secretos amnis ageret: tum gratia ruris.

Such plenty as Meredith imagined for Admetus while
Phoebus lived in his house and worked on his land Nature
heaped upon the age of gold without even the big-hearted
labour of storing mighty yields. And we, lifting up our eyes
out of our iron, or worse than iron age, vow that the grapes
are sour. Such a life must be enervating and unmanly. English
poetry and romance, indeed, have never gone to extremes in
their vision of the golden age.

> Work apace, apace, apace, apace,
> Honest labour bears a lovely face—

Dekker was a lover of the crafts, and he lived before Isaac
Watts and Samuel Smiles, and before the industrial revolution
had perverted the old 'dignity of labour' into disgrace, and
work itself into a punishment on man for daring to exist.

But the English idea of the simple life always included
activity and even toil. Polidore and Cadwal in their mountain
cave must know 'the sweat of industry', and we must suppose
their hunting spears to be tipped with iron; but Belarius has
taught them that gold and silver are 'dirty gods'. Byron will
take us several steps farther. In *Don Juan* there is a luminous
description of the simple life as lived in Daniel Boone's settle-
ment in Kentucky:

> around him grew
> A sylvan tribe of children of the chase,
> Whose young, unwakened world was ever new,
> Nor sword nor sorrow yet had left a trace
> On her unwrinkled brow, nor could you view
> A frown on Nature's or on human face;
> The free-born forest found and kept them free,
> And fresh as is a torrent or a tree.

> And tall, and strong, and swift of foot were they,
> Beyond the dwarfing city's pale abortions,
> Because their thoughts had never been the prey
> Of care or gain: the green woods were their portions;
> No sinking spirits told them they grew grey,
> No fashion made them apes of her distortions;
> Simple they were, not savage—and their rifles,
> Though very true, were not yet used for trifles.

The rifles break the primitive peace little more than the spears of the sons of Cymbeline. While the English conception of the simple life—'simple, not savage'—seems able to digest even so 'civilized' a production as a rifle, the French were—as they naturally would be—less accommodating. There were no rifles, there was no metal in that corner of the Ile de France where Virginie, and even Paul in his measure, proved by their exemplary lives that 'les lois de la nature ne sont donc que les lois de la morale universelle'. And in the famous *Discours* for the University of Dijon Rousseau dared as far as any of the dreamers of the ancient world. He pronounces against progress and civilization. He preaches 'la sainte barbarie des ancêtres, l'heureuse innocence des brutes, l'état de pure nature'— nature, who would defend men against science as a mother her child against a dangerous weapon. 'Dieu', he cries, 'délivre-nous des lumières et des funestes arts de nos pères, et rende-nous l'ignorance, l'innocence, et la pauvreté.'

Anthropology forbids us to believe in the noble savage, in the law of nature which is the moral law, even in Byron's vision of the 'simple, not savage' life. But the century and a half which separates us from the *Discours* of Rousseau has given us plenty of excuse for wishing that we might believe, and for wondering whether, after all, man is fit to be trusted with all these arts and sciences, with the machinery that they demand, and, above all, with the labour that the machinery demands. A few hours' work a day for every one, and the remaining hours for rest and leisure and self-improvement— to a world that is weary and disillusioned when it is not in actual torture, that ideal seems a makeshift, always at the mercy of circumstance, only to be achieved and maintained by unceasing adjustment of a score of personal and material forces, and so dependent upon compromise that a single violent action or self-assertive element can blow it to bits. What reason have we for thinking that, man for man, we are happier —and seeing what a mess we have made of our world of metals and machines what right have we to think that we are any more virtuous, than the idlers of the age of gold, doing at the very most a hand's turn now and then to perfect the simple life in an idealized South Sea Island, 'blue lagoon' sort of existence?

Our metals and machines have let us down. Hear their modern prophet speak:—'Law, Orrder, Duty an' Restraint, Obedience, Discipline!'—the virtues hymned by McAndrew are precisely the virtues that have produced the most frightful power for evil that the world has ever known, the virtues that give unity and system to horrors compared with which the doings of the devils in a medieval Last Judgement are but gay gambols. 'And whiles I wonder if a soul was gied them wi' the blows'—if it was, we know what sort of a soul it must be.

But there is worse to come. If we attempt to give solidity to our age of gold, we find that Nature lets us down as badly as machinery. When Diderot had indulged his fancy in the idyllic amours of Bougainville's Taiti, a commentator found in his dialogue 'plutôt une satire à la Tacite que des règles de conduite', and observed that this account of a 'nouvelle Cythère' said nothing about the infanticide there practised. Byron, keeping closer to the facts of his Kentucky, wrote:

> Motion was in their days, Rest in their slumbers,
>   And Cheerfulness the handmaid of their toil;
> Nor yet too many nor too few their numbers—

The history of the industrial revolution shows the power of machinery to raise the human birth-rate; but Bernardin's long-winded old man was right when he told Paul that, if Virginie had lived to bear him children, the simple life would have been a mighty hard life. Infanticide and leaving the sick to die—these, said Havelock Ellis, are 'the secret of the natural superiority of the savage and of the men of the old civilization'. Nature cannot be trusted; and once we cease to trust Nature, the age of gold passes out of reach. Even Shelley, poet of human perfectibility, knew that. How often must the serpent conquer the eagle before a new Laon and Cythna can bring a new and enduring age of gold? We exult in the promise in the last chorus of *Hellas*:

> The world's great age begins anew,
>   The golden years return....
> Saturn and Love their long repose
>   Shall burst, more bright and good
> Than all who fell—

and experience can never reconcile us to the last words of all:

> Oh, cease! must hate and death return?
>   Cease! must men kill and die?
> Cease! drain not to its dregs the urn
>   Of bitter prophecy.
> The world is weary of the past,
> Oh, might it die or rest at last!

He has rapt us into glory only to leave us peering in the light of Hardy's moon upon the 'show God ought to shut up soon'. And he did it deliberately in a chorus which he knew to be 'indistinct and obscure':

Prophecies of wars, and rumours of wars, etc., may safely be made by poet or prophet in any age, but to anticipate however darkly a period of regeneration and happiness is a more hazardous exercise of the faculty which bards possess or feign.

If Shelley can write like that, remembering meanwhile what precedents he has been set by Isaiah and by Virgil, it seems clear that the age of gold is not a practical consideration, and that it is only an agreeable academic interest to speculate whether it belongs to the past and will return, whether Time must 'run back' to 'fetch the age of gold', whether man has fallen from that happy state and must win his way back to it, or whether it is a new goal only to be achieved after aeons of progress. It is not, perhaps, as academic a question as it appears, because in the one case we may be 'progressing' farther and farther away from our true being, and the 'forward motion', which we so love, may be the very opposite to the 'backward steps' by which we ought to move; and in the other case, improbable though it may seem in times like these, we are working our slow and painful way in the right direction.

Faith in a golden age as a practical proposition, not absolute, indeed, but workable though finite, is not yet dead. It lived in one to whom Shelley would have allowed the 'faculty which bards possess or feign', Edward Carpenter. For him, too, the break-up of the age of gold began with 'auri sacra fames'—the growth of wealth and the conception of private property. It is not easy to recognize our neolithic, or even our remoter palaeolithic, friends in the idyllic light. It is even less easy to see in 'sandals and sun-bathing' the first steps forward out of civilization—that disease the cure of which is to fetch back the age of gold, the 'sainte barbarie des ancêtres'.

> Omnis feret omnia tellus.
> Non rastros patietur humus, non vinea falcem,
> Robustus quoque iam tauris iuga solvet arator.

That is exceedingly unlikely. Yet one feature of that age there is in which Carpenter is at one with Virgil:

> Ante Jovem . . .
> ne signare quidem aut partiri limite campum
> fas erat: in medium quaerebant, ipsaque tellus
> omnia liberius, nullo poscente ferebat.

There will be no more private ownership of land, with its corollaries of landless men, rent, mortgage interest, and so forth; and rumours of that return are beating on our ears more loudly and in higher earnest than any sandals and sun-bathing.

Suppose that it is all a dream, that there never was an age of gold and never will be? Suppose that nature—even communistically cultivated—will always be man's enemy, and that the primrose path and the factory-lined trunk road both lead to destruction, we need not on that account 'lose our Eden', our Atlantis, our age of gold, past or future. To cherish it at heart is, at the least, to keep the idea of human personality distinct from the idea of mechanical compulsion. The machines will never get us down so long as, during our short span of life, we keep our souls our own. And we can take no harm from holding before us the unattainable ideal of peace on earth to men of good will, which would be the universal reality in a world where all men were naturally good.

EPHEMERA

THE HOTEL THAT MOVED

(1924)

The train was a fast train—so fast that it seemed now and then to be on the point of rattling and rocking itself right over. One passenger, at least, felt that he had had enough of movement for a while. And then came the necessary drive to the destination. It was a long drive. The taxicab was even more of a rattle-trap than the train. And its way went across railway-lines that stuck for inches above the ground, over thick ropes, through deep holes in which the water gleamed grey and greasy under the grey and greasy sky, into and out of sheds, round sharp corners, and half into, half out of morasses. Not all the devilments in the amusements ground at Wembley, I believed, could leave one feeling so shaken as I felt when at last I stopped in front of the building where I was to meet and part from my friend.

It was an enormous building. It towered huge in windowed tier on tier above the dwarfed sheds. Massive, mountainous, it proclaimed solidity. Here at last was something firm, and something that kept still. With profound relief I felt the ground once more beneath my feet, as I went up to the first floor, and down a long, white, brilliantly lighted corridor on a thick, soft carpet, towards my friend's room. I passed across an enormous landing, out of which opened a gay-looking dining-room. Everywhere there were attentive and obliging men-servants—some of them a little masterful, maybe, in manner, but all as alert to help and guide as possible. I saw electric signs showing the way to the swimming-bath, the gymnasium, the library, the lounge, and many other such features of good hotel life. At a desk in one corner a very capable gentleman in dark blue was allotting tables for meals to a chatting string of guests, so that there might be none of that jealousy about such things which is common in large hotels. I could not but admire the quickness and silence with which the servants were handling luggage. Everywhere comfort, everywhere solidity and an air of repose, in spite of the bustle. And cheerful, serene repose was the note struck at first sight by my friend's room—a bed-sitting room, small, but quite large enough, and very prettily furnished with tables, chairs, a sofa, all sorts of bookshelves and cupboards and things. And to one who had another drive to the station and another journey to London before him, that deep, cosy bed looked inexpressibly inviting. Tea? It was brought in a moment, very daintily served. I settled down in my chair with a delicious sense of peace, of solidity, of immobility. In that huge, massive building, what could there be but quiet and stillness?

And an hour later the whole colossal thing began to move. I saw it. Standing alongside it and peering up its neck-breaking height, I watched it moving. It was incredible. If Bush House suddenly began moving up Kingsway, it could seem no stranger. My solid, comfortable, peaceful hotel, refuge from the pains of journeying, repose for jolted bones and aching muscles, was itself moving, was itself indeed an instrument of motion. It had seemed so still; its purpose was to move. It had seemed so huge; that evening someone from cliff or lighthouse would see it looking quite small. In a day or two it would be a walnut shell on an ocean, a tiny toy of a thing to be rolled this way and that, heaved up and sent plunging down, twisted and slapped and pushed, and only defying by its own power of motion forces that could otherwise tear it to pieces. Those solid, comforting floors would suddenly strike or elude the feet that sought them. The white dainty walls would reel. The comfortable silence would change to creaking, groaning, banging; and my harbour of refuge from the strain of movement would be itself all strain, all movement, until from harbour it had made harbour and could once more for awhile lie at rest. I felt a little more kindly even to the taxi-cab; and the train-journey on solid ground seemed luxurious.

A HILL-TOP LUNCH

(1938)

The hotel porter condescended to have heard of that remote village; there were two places where you might get lunch, one right at the bottom, the other right at the top. The travellers were hot and hungry by the time they reached the inn at the bottom, but neither of them appeared to see it.

There are eating places which, on a holiday, one simply does not use—they are so dull. It must be the place at the top, then, or no lunch this day except the chocolate (by now probably a little soft) in their pockets. For elderly legs and defective breathing it was 20 minutes' hard grind up to the top of that village, which from afar off on the other side of the valley had seemed to slope so gently to the foot of the gigantic cliff. Now by cobbled inclines and now by long flights of stone stairs the way led up and up, bending and twisting between the gleaming white walls, past orange trees and lemon trees on which only the eye might refresh itself, while the ear was enchanted and the throat mocked by the perpetual music of mountain water running down the open channels. But here at last was the cramped little medieval gate, and a final effort up sunless streets brought them into a new blaze of sunlight falling (O blessed sight!) upon a space of flat ground.

It was perhaps 20 yards square, and it contained several small tables, three burly, nail-booted climbers just down from the top of the cliff, one little girl, and a round dozen of dogs. The travellers sank down at a table on the edge of the platform. No need to tell each other that they had done right to climb. The table-cloth, and the huge, limp, white table-napkins, like face towels, proclaimed the right thing. And before they had begun to take in the beauty of the wide view up to the crags and down to the seaward valleys, a brisk woman was at their side, and they were talking about *hors d'œuvres* (that meant radishes and olives and sausage with garlic in it), and omelettes, and veal cutlets, and cheese, and about things to drink—about beer from Monaco, and huge, corkless bottles of red wine of the country. In no time talk had changed into act; and that was when the strangeness first took hold of the travellers. There was no one to do for them but the woman and (it seemed a sort of joke at first, but not for long) the child. She was the waitress. Her age was six, her sense of responsibility very grave. With meticulous care (*meticulous* because she really was afraid—afraid of disgracing herself by dropping something), with ceremonial slowness she brought bottles and glasses, or piled up used plates and laboured off with the load. Soon the company was increased by two French women and one bad-tempered old man; but mother and daughter never grew rattled. With precise efficiency they went on supplying the guests with food that was as good as it was well served. There was even time, over the omelette, for a chat with the cook. It began with the dogs, sprawling all over the place in the dead, sunbaked stillness. No, they were not her dogs, drat them! They belonged to the sportsmen, the hunters. The village was full of hunters—there were more hunters than game. And so on, under the touch of feminine sympathy, to more intimate troubles. Her husband had gone off again, and she had no one to help her but the little girl.

It was just then that a corner of the table-cloth fluttered up. Three minutes later the little square was empty. Cook, waitress, guests, dogs, and all had run for shelter out of the wind and the dust. Unperturbed, the staff continued to serve the meal indoors instead of out; and the cross old man was allowed to curse the climate unreproved. As the travellers struggled down the hill, hats were flying, dust came spinning round corners to smother them; the cold was bitter. And for three days the mistral screamed and raged over the land.

That night, once more down on the Blue Coast, the travellers were dining in luxury. Servitors in white and servitors in black sped silently on thick carpets; food and drink appeared as if by magic. The scene was worthy of the pen of Mr E. Phillips Oppenheim, and fifty mistrals could not have disturbed its mellow richness. But it all seemed unreal. What was vivid and actual was a small Provençale of six, half amused and half awestruck at the discovery that, if a kind English lady gives you (O incredible treasure!) a square of chocolate which is made up of four small squares lightly joined together, you can break it across, not only *this* way, but also *that* way.

TROPICAL FAUNA: A TIGER, A RABBIT, AND OTHERS
(1928)

At the fourth tee the Tiger stopped addressing his ball, and held up his hand. 'Listen,' he said, 'that's monkeys.' The Rabbit, with his ears full of the queer, clinking, chattering noise, peered hard into the forest; but no more than a couple of yards away the *Matto*, the jungle vegetation, was so thick that no eye could pierce it. Somewhere parakeets were screaming; but they, too, were invisible.

The Tiger made a lovely shot. A hundred and fifty feet or so below, the green was just within sight. His ball cleared the tops of the queresma trees, a flaunting mass of purple, fell short of the banana grove and rolled on to the green—rolled just a thought too far and disappeared over the edge. The Tiger growled; and well he might, seeing that his ball must either be caught by a stone on an almost perpendicular slope or lying 30 or 40 feet below the green at the bottom of a rocky stream. The Rabbit did what he always does with an iron club. His sliced ball tumbled ignominiously into some long grass. His caddie, who had posted himself near it with quite disgusting prescience, leaped into the air with a yell. The boy's face, being permanently boot-black, could not be said to go pale; but his eyes and teeth were like fireworks and he gibbered like a squirrel. Even ears unused to Portuguese could catch one awful word—'Cobra!'

The Tiger said nothing, but was mighty quick on the spot. 'No harm done,' he said, when he had examined the bare foot which the urchin was clasping, 'It did not bite him, only went over his instep. They call all snakes "cobra", and very likely it wasn't poisonous.'

To get to the fifth tee you have to cross the stream into which the Tiger's ball had rolled. At a point about 20 yards lower down, the plank lies close to some big stones, partly in and partly out of the shallow water; and the players were just setting foot on it when the Tiger stopped dead. 'Look!' he whispered, pointing to a patch of water shaded by a stone. The glare of the sun was so fierce that at first the Rabbit could see nothing in the shade. He had not long to wait. The beast came out into the light—seven or eight feet of it, its body coiling about and about on the gravelly bottom of the shallow stream, its devilish head up in air and its forked tongue flickering like the very spirit of hate. The caddies were gibbering like anything. 'Venenosissimo!' 'It is that,' said the Tiger; 'it's one of the worst.' And, armed with his heaviest iron, he began clambering down into the bed of the stream. It looked as if the snake meant to wait for him; and mortally glad was the Rabbit when, having had a good look at that club and the man behind it, it swished suddenly round and disappeared under a great stone, where it could be neither seen nor reached. A nice thing for a Rabbit who was used to no fauna on a golf-course but his white-scutted brothers and a sheep or so!

It may be because of the snakes—it may be only because from the stream to the fifth tee it is a very steep little climb; but at any rate, just this side of the tee there is a very pretty thatched hut where ice may be heard to tinkle and liquid to go guggle-guggle. To every man his fancy; but your fate at the fifth hole depends entirely (supposing that you carry the stream —and the snakes) on whether you do or do not get among the mango trees. And, as the majestic great green and brown mangoes, massed in their deep hollow, are on the right of the high-towering green, the Rabbit had declined a drink in vain.

The Tiger did the hole in 2, one under bogey; for, as a player remarked, many of these nine holes are pretty easy 3's and very difficult 11's. Well, well! With the thermometer at 95 it is an achievement for English rabbits to play these nine at all. And then the swim in the great fresh-water bathing pool; and more tinklings and gugglings on the verandah of the old, long, low, cool Brazilian farmhouse which is now the club house; and the view seaward to the islands, and the view landward to the mountain striking with his noble bald head the tropical sky in which the vultures wheel, his mighty shoulders mantled in the green and gold and purple and white of the everlasting jungle—this is golf at Gavea near Rio. Rabbits may well find it more difficult than ever to keep their eyes on that wretched little white object; but no Tigers in the world are so friendly and so encouraging as the Tigers of Gavea.

THREE PASSES

(1924)

To think that it was only a fortnight ago that we sprang from our beds at five o'clock in the morning, swallowed scalding coffee in a shuttered *salle-à-manger* smelling strong of last night's dinner, and tripped over housemaids and rolls of carpet on our way to the front door, where already, in the dim light, the little fellow was waiting! The little fellow has a wheel at each corner, the heart of a lion, and some first-rate brakes; and we made calls on them all before the day was out. Dawn changed to daylight as we skimmed along the lake shore, where fawn-coloured cows wagged their bells at us and peasants stared at the mad English who were up and about when they might have been in bed. This must be Brunnen, and this Flüelen; and still, as we spin up the valley, we who are not at the wheel are but half-awake. Now we are at Gösschenen, where the St Gothard tunnel opens its grim mouth; but we can spare only a glance for Devil's Bridges and such postcard subjects. Up we go, and into a cloud that promises excitement, perhaps disappointment, to come; and through the cloud into Andermatt, wide-awake in the sunshine. We too are wide-awake; for Andermatt means more coffee, and already we are hungry as hunters.

The little fellow is in excellent trim and seems eager to be off. Here is Hospenthal with its old tower; and, leaving the St Gotthard pass on the left, we murmur: 'Now we are for it!' We swing away to the right, for the Furka is our aim, the Furka Pass, which is only 10 ft. short of 8,000 ft. high; and ahead of us looms another monstrous cloud, as still, it seems, as if it were waiting there on purpose to spoil the fun. The little fellow, masterly driven, makes short work of it. We are above the stupid thing. Very soon we are above the trees. Rocks, harebells of a profound and noble blue, whortleberry-plants (are they not?) crimsoning huge stretches of the solitude. Is there anyone in the world besides ourselves? Indeed there is. Round the sharp corner of a rock comes a noble chestnut horse, and on his back as handsome an officer as any army in the world can show. He signals to us imperiously; and the little fellow, who had really seemed to be bolting with us, so gaily did he swing round hairpins at a gradient of one in three, must humbly stand on the precipice-edge—the wrong side of the road too!—while past us down the hill trails a half-mile or more of wagons and soldiers and searchlights and horses and guns.

The road is clear again, and off we go. Desolation becomes more desolate as we leave even the bluebells and the whortle-berries behind, and see all about us snowfields and black crags and the steely gleam of blue ice. It becomes dream-like, this endless climbing and twisting. The sun is high; we have a roof over our heads; yet it is bitter cold. And then, suddenly, we are at the top. The little fellow begins to pull more madly than ever; and before we have grasped our joy, he has con-descended to draw up at the great grim hotel.

We have climbed the Furka; but the thrill of that not so

very modest achievement is swept clean away at the turn of
the road by the first sight of the Rhone Glacier. Everybody
knows the Rhone Glacier. As we stare at it, here come, from
the other direction, two great motor-cars, puffing and roaring
in a way of which the little fellow would be ashamed; and
there are other tourists in dozens staring as we are staring.
Yet can the tenth, the hundredth sight of the Rhone Glacier
be any less thrilling than the first? The cruel, beautiful thing,
from the fairy pinnacles of its top to the sordid mess at its base,
which its remorseless teeth have ground out of the mountains,
and the stream of thick, whitey-blue ice water that trickles
ghastly from its foot—the brighter the sun gleams on it, the
more cruel seems its beauty. Turn from it before it puts a spell
on you, and look up into the moving clouds beyond the valley.
There the lovely Weisshorn heaves its monstrous shoulder;
and there—there—just on the left of it, incredibly higher still,
that is the black, the dreadful peak of Matterhorn.

It is on coming down the Furka towards Gletsch that a
timid soul is most likely to wish himself safe in the Kursaal
at Lucerne, and to marvel at the heroic people who trust
themselves here in charabancs, in any car with a long wheel-
base. There goes the road down, like a twisted white ribbon,
to that speck in the abyss which is Gletsch; and there from
Gletsch up it goes again over the Grimsel. Even the little
fellow seems to set his teeth as he begins to tackle that anything
but facile descent. But—in such hands as these—he is a
wonder for taking corners, and for going steadily down and
up; and very soon—too soon, we feel, so quickly is the day
passing—we are half-way up the Grimsel. A punster would
have said that the pass was well named. Grim, indeed, it is,
far grimmer though lower than the Furka; and the sell was
awaiting us at the top—a cloud that swallowed us alive. Of
the Dead Lake we saw but the bleak edge; of the road but a
yard or two; of the view nothing. Ghostly rocks crawled into
sight and slunk out of sight. After the brightness of the sun-
smitten Furka the desolation was appalling. And so down,
down, we groped our way; and we were down among the

fir-trees again before the sky lifted; and amid the noise of
many waters the little fellow's brakes might cool down, and
three chilly men, empty indeed, but almost too excited to be
hungry, unpacked the baskets.

A pause, of course, for the Handeck Falls; and then for the
Brünig Pass and home. The Brünig? Pooh! a mere trifle to
a little fellow who has done the Furka and the Grimsel. Why,
it never gets above the trees! As we glided by the man who
was calling the cows home through a horn some twelve foot
long, we fancied ourselves already at the top. And, after all,
it was the Brünig at which the little fellow jibbed. Taken that
way, it seems, the Brünig is much steeper than the trees allow
it to look; and it needed a deal of coaxing and a mile or so of
very salubrious walking before our gallant little friend found
his troubles over and could trot us quickly along the lake-side
home; our bodies weary, our minds teeming with memories
of a day of fun, of splendour, of beauty, of awe.

Worse luck, you cannot pat a motor-car and give it a bran-
mash or a lump of sugar. But it will bring me something like
the same feeling of a debt paid if I am allowed to say that the
gallant little fellow is technically called a Sedan, and is named
—after his maker—Henry.

THE REAL MRS BEETON
(1932)

Mrs Beeton lived in the Victorian era, which, as every one
under 30 knows, was dismally frumpish. She wrote about
cookery and household management; and, as the Principal of
an English Training College said the other day in a lecture on
education, 'Girls are to be educated as human beings, not as
potential housewives. In any case, cooking is an affair which
a woman can always hire someone else to do for her, while she
devotes her time to higher interests.' It stands to reason, then,
that Mrs Beeton must have been a frump, with no higher

interests. And there she sits, in the popular imagination, middle-aged, stout, in black bombazine, wearing a cap and a stern, if kindly, expression, domestic, quite definitely unintellectual.

She was nothing of the sort. Her youngest son has portraits of her as a very pretty child and as a beautiful young woman, with a face that indicates her keen intelligence. And there are people still living who remember Isabella Mary Mayson as a lovely girl of 20 when, in 1856, she married Samuel Orchardt Beeton, editor and publisher, who was also young and equally good-looking. To her numerous half-brothers and sisters the new brother whom Isabella gave them was a veritable hero of romance. The description of her wedding-gown has been preserved in a letter written years afterwards by one of those young sisters. 'She wore a white silk dress trimmed with little flounces from waist to hem, and a large white bonnet and veil!'

And she never grew old. She was only 29 when she died, in 1865, two days after the birth of her fourth son, now Sir Mayson Beeton.

When they were first married Mr and Mrs Beeton lived at 284, Strand, where the new Law Courts now stand. Mrs Beeton was in reality a journalist, and a very good one, with a fine literary style. She and her husband worked together. He edited and published, among a vast number of other things, a journal called *The Englishwoman's Domestic Magazine*; and in this journal Mrs Beeton wrote the fashion articles as well as those on household management. She must have begun collecting materials for her now famous book almost immediately on her marriage. It was issued originally in 24 monthly parts at 3*d.* each, the first number appearing on 1 October 1859; and in the preface to the first edition in book form, published in 1861, she says that it was the result of four years' incessant labour. What moved her to undertake it was

the discomfort and suffering which I had seen brought upon men and women by household mismanagement. I have always thought that there is no more fruitful source of family discontent than a

The Real Mrs Beeton

housewife's badly-cooked dinners and untidy ways. Men are now so well served out of doors—at their clubs, well-ordered taverns and dining-houses—that, in order to compete with the attractions of these places, a mistress must be thoroughly acquainted with the theory and practice of cookery,

as well as with the other arts of making and keeping a comfortable home. But that was not all. 'In the department belonging to the Cook I have striven...to make my work something more than a Cookery-Book.'

She succeeded. Parts of her book are good literature, and, besides being a contribution to the social history of her time, it abounds in curious learning and various information. Before we come to the recipe for fried anchovies (the first of the fish) we may read of fish in general that

in the eyes of the heroes of Homer it had little favour; for Menelaus complained that 'hunger pressed their digestive organs', and they had been obliged to live on fish. Subsequently, however, fish became one of the principal articles of diet among the Hellenes; and both Aristophanes and Athenaeus allude to it, and even satirize their countrymen for their excessive partiality to the turbot and mullet.

And since we have minds as well as stomachs it is well that, before we so much as begin to pluck our bird, we may read a few admirably expressed paragraphs of general observations on birds as living beings, which can both fly and sing. So thorough was Mrs Beeton's work that her bereaved husband, adding a note to the preface to the edition of 1869, could say: 'The arrangement of the first edition was so well conceived that it admitted of scarcely any reform; and my late wife's writing was so clear and her directions were so practical that only the slightest alterations and corrections were needed, except such as Time had rendered necessary.'

Mr Beeton, who had always suffered from pulmonary trouble, survived his wife for some 12 years and died in 1877. Before that *Mrs Beeton's Cookery-Book* had passed out of his possession, and the family has now no financial interest in it. But the book in its original form remains one of the classics of our age—the work of a young, beautiful, highly cultivated woman doomed to early death.

MEALS IN THE TRAIN

(1923)

One of the first truths to be learned from the study of aesthetics is that the nature of the material, the exciting cause, of pleasure goes for very little in the composition of that pleasure. It is what we bring, not what we receive (as Coleridge pointed out in an ode on dejection which is among the finest of hymns to joy), which makes us glad or sorry. An instance of this great philosophical truth is within easy reach of every traveller; and most of us are travellers at this time of the year. No one—not even the master caterers of the great railway companies, whose new names are still as strange to us as was the wife's new name to the angry husband in *Modern Love*—would lay hand on heart and swear that in respect of quality the meals served in the luncheon cars of our long-distance trains were choice food. Considering the difficulties, they are surprisingly sound; usually well cooked, cleanly dished, and deftly served by obliging waiters, who combine the skill of Cinquevalli and of Blondin with the affability of the old fellow in *You Never Can Tell*. But there is nearly always turbot, or cod—fishes that, when they take the train or stay in a hotel, become as uninteresting, as reserved, as flatly respectable as English travellers themselves. The choice between roast joint hot and pressed beef or ham cold seems no choice at all, but a double compulsion, as of pistols or swords to a timid duellist. And the meal, unlike all other meals, be it luncheon or be it dinner, strikes one as drawing slowly *crescendo* to a climax of sweetish biscuits and gorgonzola cheese. Why is there nearly always gorgonzola cheese in the train; and why does one always eat and enjoy it there, and rarely anywhere else?

We have hit, perhaps, on one of the qualities which we bring of ourselves to the enjoyment of meals in the train. We bring our sense that we are doing something unusual, and we lend it to the usual food. The most frequent traveller (if we except the commercial traveller, who, as a rule, avoids the restaurant-car) has more meals in a house than in the train. There is always a spice of the adventurous, or at least the unfamiliar, in eating while food and fork and mouth and gastric juices are all sensibly moving at half-a-hundred miles an hour. True, railway restaurant-cars are all very much alike; one soon becomes dulled to the difference between white panelling touched with gold and brown panelling inlaid with yellow, and all restaurant-cars seem to have windows that will neither open nor shut. But still, none of them is our own dining-room; the plates are not our plates; the spoons are not those we use daily. And the adventure reaches its height when we try to pour out our ginger-ale while the train is going over points. And how ready we are for adventure! While we dutifully work through the turbot, the joint, and the roast potatoes, counting the courses till we reach the sweetish biscuits and the gorgonzola, the world fleets by us; no real world, but a panorama unrolled for our delectation, with no lecturer to interrupt its flow. Some people like to eat to music, which saves them the mental effort of talking. Better than music is the rhythm of the wheels (which men of science declare to be as much our own doing as is the pleasure of railway menus), that rhythm which comes to seem the very tune of the landscape as it circles past our idle, interested eyes, swinging on the pivot of some distant wood or church or hill-top. And there are the stopping-places, always bestowing a thrill which meals in houses cannot give. Will anyone get into our carriage? Will he or she or they see through the sham of the coats and bags which we have arranged with so much artful carelessness on the empty places? Could it be, O horror! that this ordinary-looking station harbours railway thieves who will make off with our hand luggage? Or the train may be making headlong for London; the first suburbs have been already penetrated, and it is a question whether the dinner will be done before the journey. Quick! let us finish our gorgonzola cheese and pay the bill and go. After all, is this restaurant-car really as alluring as we thought?

LA CRÉATRICE DE CAMEMBERT
(1927)

Yesterday in pleasant Normandy, the country of orchards and of dairies, honour was paid, with proper French ceremony and proper French pride, to a woman who in her day did good service to France and to humanity. Marie Harel (*née* Fontaine), who was born in 1761, was the inventor—the *créatrice*, as her countrymen nobly call it—of the Camembert cheese. Near the farm at Camembert, where she made the first Camembert cheese, a monument was unveiled, and in Vimoutiers, the neighbouring town, a street has been named after her. The honours are deserved; and many English men and women, who know what is good to eat and what France has done for good eating, will be glad to learn the news. Charles Dickens, Charles Lever, and Charles Lamb—any of these three would be worthy to celebrate the praise of Camembert cheese, for all three had the gift of enjoying good food and the art to make their readers feel how good it was. Had Lamb been privileged to taste the cheese of Camembert, would he have classed it with 'the popular minions that absolutely court you', or would he have allowed it 'the reserved collegiate worth' of brawn? That partly depends upon whether he waited till it was ripe—*coulant* is the correct phrase. Too many English eaters treat Camembert cheese as they treat bananas (and as they would no doubt treat medlars, were fresh-picked medlars masticable by any jaws but pigs'), and fall upon it when it is still immature and tasteless. Camembert cheese, indeed, deserves no less consideration than a fine pear: one should be ready to sit up all night with it, as the saying is, in order to make sure of the moment of perfection. The pressed English cheeses—Stilton, double Gloucester, Cheddar, Cheshire, and the now too rare, delicious 'blue vinny' of Dorset—are eaten, as a rule, too soon. The unpressed cheeses (and among them Brie should be named with honour, even at a moment when all thoughts are fixed on Camembert), the cheeses which need a knife and care in the handling, are, for English eaters, delicacies; and never should they be cut short in the flower of their youth and hurried to an untimely end.

'How do apples get into dumplings?' demanded King George III; but, when enlightened, he did not go on to ask who first thought of building the dumpling round the apple. Who invented bubble-and-squeak? Who put mint sauce with lamb (it was merely lemon juice when Peacock's parsons were hearty at their victuals)? Who brought the red-currant jelly to the mutton; and to what towering genius do we owe fried steak and onions? It may, indeed, be that their names are recorded in the archives of cookery; but for mankind in general they have suffered the fate from which France, as eminent in *pietas* as in gastronomy, has rescued Mme Harel; they have no memorial; they are perished, as though they had never been. Experts know well who invented this or that apolaustic confection. Yet to see—in the caves, say, near Mentone—the bones which primitive man threw over his shoulder when he had gnawed them, is to marvel first how he learned the effect of fire upon flesh, and next at the incalculable difference between the cooking of primitive man and the dishes seen to-day upon our tables. His roast beef, we may be sure, was not as ours; and certainly he had no Yorkshire pudding to eat with it. Mme Harel comes high up in the scale. Behind her she had aeons of cheese-making, through which we may peer in vain for the man or woman who made the first cheese. And, as Major Segrave's motor-car goes by at more than 200 miles an hour, we may wonder who it was that made the first wheel. The wonder runs through all the activities of man; and, when we join with France in honouring Mme Harel and her delicious cheese, we may spare a thought of gratitude to all the unknown benefactors who have helped to make cheese, and human life, as good as they are.

METAPHORICALLY SPEAKING
(1931)

According to the report, an escaped convict, recaptured on Tuesday, said to the police: 'I am hungry and fed up'; and probably neither he nor the policemen were just then aware that they had witnessed a small but definite event in the history of the English language. Hungry and fed up—it is impossible to be both at once, if the words are taken literally; and never before, perhaps, has there been so sharp an instance of self-contradiction. Yet the speaker meant something comprehensible, and the hearers are more likely to have understood his meaning at once than to have seen the irreconcilable contradiction in the words. And suppose that he had desired to be more emphatic, and had said 'I am hungry and literally fed up', how many readers of the sentence in the newspapers would have seen anything wrong? Very few, we suspect; because 'fed up' has long been losing any literal meaning it may once have had. Many a soldier wrote home from the front to say that he was fed up with the War, but that the food was very good. The time was sure to come when that phrase 'fed up' would lose all association with material feeling; and come it apparently has.

The kinds and causes of change in language are many. One kind is suggested by the word 'literally', used above. Before long 'literally' will only mean its true opposite, 'metaphorically'—much as 'prevent' has come to mean 'obstruct' instead of 'lead forward'—and when 'littery gents' write of 'a certain' this or that they nearly always mean an uncertain. But the history of 'fed up' is the history of one among many metaphors that have become so common as no longer to suggest their origin and their literal meaning. Other examples are easy to find. 'Where on earth have you dropped from?' That is, or used to be, a common expression; and few that used it would observe that they had spoiled a metaphor, because the original force of 'dropped from' was to suggest some strange, far place—a cloud, a sunbeam, a star, anything so long as it was not 'on earth'. Some metaphors are so convenient that they become (to use one of them that is already a good deal distorted) catchwords; and even experienced writers may miss their force. In a very earnest article about humane slaughter it was stated not long ago that 'those who advocate the abandonment of the pole-axe in favour of the humane killer had no axe to grind'; and of an athlete whose foot was amputated it was said that his career as a runner was cut short. This deadness to the origin and meaning of metaphors leads not only to the dusty jargon of politics—the ships of state, the unsheathed swords, the clouds on the horizon—but also to the exploration of avenues and other unusual proceedings to which politicians seem to be addicted. There is no use in being pedantic. The human mind cannot express itself without metaphor; and nearly every sentence spoken or written must contain at least one. For most people it is better to say that they are fed up, and get on with their work, than to spend time wondering how Dr Johnson would have put it or hunting for other expressions, every one of which would probably turn out to be in origin metaphorical. But there are powers of preservation at work. One is undoubtedly the right sort of crossword puzzle (the wrong sort greatly increases the dulling of metaphor), which directs attention to the composition, history, and meaning of words. Another is those lovers of language, who do their best to stem the tide or put on the brake or hold the fort; those who are thoroughly fed up with all this abuse or metaphor (perhaps so fed up as to be utterly sick of it); and, even when they are as hungry as hunters and as cross as two sticks, had rather die than drop a brick.

TAILORS AND MEN
(1924)

A hundred years ago, as a quotation in our columns recorded yesterday, the tailors' foremen of London met at the White Horse Tavern, in Regent Street, to proceed with the formation of a kind of union. Their honourable craft was being invaded by speculators who knew nothing of its *arcana*; and the foremen met to protect the responsibility and the respectability of their order. In the report of the meeting we can still trace the indignation of the artist against the man of mere commerce. Echoes of the speeches made can be heard to-day in what the actors say about the theatrical syndicates; what architects may be heard to mutter about municipal councils. One speaker in particular had the ear of the assembly. If he cut coats as well as he made speeches, he must have been valuable to his employer, for the report shows that he could stitch humour on to indignation and make his hearers laugh as well as steel their bosoms in the cause. He fell back upon the old saying that nine tailors make a man (if his arithmetic was not at fault, he even put the insult in the proportion not of nine, but of ten to one). And he declared, in Shylock's vein, that a foreman tailor had the dimensions, passions, appetites, and spirit of a man. Hath not a Jew eyes? Hath not a foreman tailor a tongue to make droll and daring speeches with? It was all the masters' fault. And the masters were not men; they were individuals. How many individuals make a man we do not read that he reckoned, thereby missing almost as good a point as Dickens missed in the matter of the tomato and the love-apple. But he spoke so bravely and with so much more than the ninth part of a man's humour, that one would gladly know the upshot of the affair. Were the *profanum vulgus* driven out from the *arcana*? Or did the tailors only cook their goose?

There was one other point that the speaker appears to have missed: a sense—doubtless Teufelsdröckhian, but not yet

169

shop-soiled—in which nine, and probably many more, tailors make a man. In a story now many years old two small boys were promised by their tutor (he was not Mr Barlow, we believe) a plum-pudding which it had taken a thousand men to make. When Christmas Day came the deluded youngsters saw a pudding of indifferent size, and must listen to the pedant's discourse on all the labour that had gone to the making of it, since the corn was sown and the raisins were on the vine. How many tailors it took to make Beau Brummel or the Prince Regent is past calculation; but it must take more than nine to make the quietly well-dressed man of to-day. Put us into an ill-fitting coat (that is, a coat that never did fit, not a good fit now shapeless), or a pair of trousers too long or too short, and we are indeed not our full selves. We crawl apologetic where we should walk like men. See, too, the ruthlessness with which the fitter will slash to pieces a coat which the three mirrors show our untutored eyes to be faultless, and realize how much pains and *limae labor* go to the making of the confidence which is more than half our comfort. And the art of the tailor is not only an art of scissors and needles and thread. He rivals the doctor in beneficent deceit, the club secretary in patient urbanity. Our figure, he assures us, has not altered a half-inch these five years; and while he speaks he is framing his secret orders for the expanded waist-line and the little extra ease over the shoulders. Thoughtless, ungrateful, we walk the streets careless of our debt to the artist and the subtle counsellor for his share in this feeling that we are fine fellows who can look the world in the face. And perhaps we are wise not to know too much of his art. For some people a knowledge of astronomy robs the stars of their influence; for others the science of music is a foe to its emotional effect. In 'No. 5, John Street' the young gentleman knew all about 'scies' and such mysteries; but in his case this, indeed, was knowledge that 'oppressed with surfeit, and soon turned Wisdom to folly'. It is both nobler and safer to reverence the *arcana* of the sacred Nine.

SCIENTIFIC COMFORT
(1932)

An innocent-looking little article published in this issue under the title 'Measuring Comfort of Rooms' will disclose to the wary reader a new move in the ruthless, relentless, remorseless advance of the tyranny of science. We have long been used to being told what was good for us, and meekly accepting what we were told. Doctors, nurses, chemists, and other such authorized bullies, having first found out what each man likes best, have declared it bad for him, and with a more than Bolshevist heartlessness have taken it away from him. But up to the present there has been no humbug about consulting the tastes of their victims. Broiled lobster, port, very hot baths, cigarettes, and others of life's gentler pleasures have been forbidden, but on the open grounds of their bad effects, not on the hypocritical plea that the cowering wretch did not enjoy them. Yet so long as five years ago one particular kind of scientific research was prepared to state in mathematical terms what 'thermal comfort' was—in other words to tell every one, by hard-and-fast rules, without asking anyone's opinion, when his room was too hot or too cold for his liking, too damp or too dry, and all that sort of thing. Never was collectivization carried to more tyrannous lengths; never were personal taste and feeling more insolently flouted. Science might as well tell a man in mathematical terms that he likes Bombay duck or jazz music or purple finger-nails, or any of the things which some people heartily love and others fiercely detest. Science, forsooth, to tell us when we are comfortable and when we are not, without asking our opinion? The idea is intolerable.

It is too late to protest. The instrument for measuring comfort, as the article states, has been invented and approved; and in a few years not a plain, homely man will dare to say that he likes a good 'frowst', not a fresh-air fiend will dare to open the windows and set all the other people's teeth chattering. The machine will tell them both when they are 'comfortable', and after a few sharp Luddite incidents the world will settle down into its usual tame obedience. Fortunate then (or unfortunate, according to the individual view of the 'sorrow's crown of sorrow') they who can recall past days and nights in which they were allowed to decide for themselves when they were comfortable. They will summon up remembrance of the childish joy of breaking the ice in the jug on a winter morning, in the days when winter was winter; certain great open fires in old country houses with huge tongs and long curved pokers to pull the logs about with; schoolroom tea with toast making in front of the red heart of the fire; the satisfaction of doing a good morning's work in a room that was warm enough for the worker just because it was much too hot for anyone who came heartily and breezily in from outside—all sorts of smiling memories of temperatures far on this side or on that of science's mathematically defined thermal comfort. And when science, with its unruffled and exasperating pertinacity, sticks to its point and declares that that is all very well, but that comfort implies not adventurous extremes and changes, but a mean so stable that it induces unconsciousness of heat or cold, any man will still be at liberty to grumble that his particular mean is very much above or below that prescribed by the machine. But science is sure to win the argument; because when its opponent grows heated in the discussion the machine will be there to show him up, and to shame him back into 'comfort'. We had all better surrender with a good grace, and only beg for a short respite before science invents a machine to tell us what books we like and a machine to betray to us our true taste in the opposite sex.

THE FUTURE OF CARTOPHILY

(1939)

An article in this journal yesterday explains why poor children
have given up asking, 'Got a cigarette picture, Mister?'—or,
quite as frequently, 'Lady?' The cause was not, as good
citizens hoped, an improvement in public manners and elementary education. It was despair of getting what they asked for.
Cigarette cards have become meat for their masters; and what
once had been inconsidered trifles, fit only for the brief fancies
of childhood or for 'the raven's foolish hoard', are now coveted,
collected, classified, catalogued, and commercialized by grown
and serious men. We read already of 'odds specialists' in
cartophily (there is the new word, all pat) and of dealers in
mint sets. We shall hear before long of 'conditions-men', and
there will be picksome Pierpont Morgans, for whom the best
is scarcely good enough, and omnivorous Folgers, who buy by
quantity and weight. He that finds a cigarette card quite
definitely dated 1882 will win among cartophilists renown
equal to his that shall find a skull older than the Piltdown, or
whatever known skull may be older than that. Whether the
piece he rescues from the oblivion of that hoary antiquity be
the portrait of some prehistoric actor or actress—'Henry
Irving, Ellen Terry, or Letty Lind', not to mention George
Alexander, Adelaide Ristori, or Louie Freear—or whether
it shows W. G. with beard and bat, or Thomas Atkins in
Victorian uniform, or the dairy in St James's Park, or a
Metropolitan horse omnibus with the umbrella above the
driver, his fame will surely spread beyond front page news in
The Ciragette Card. His portrait and his unique piece will
appear, opposite a Titian or an Epstein, in the *Magpie Magazine*; and the British Museum, the Victoria and Albert, and
the National Art-Collections Fund will begin to keep an eye
on him.

Those alert and wide-minded institutions are probably

taking all the necessary steps already. Or does the duty rather fall on more directly academic bodies? Should this or that patron and benefactor of sound learning be approached in the matter of founding a chair of cartophily in the University of London? For there can be no questioning the educational value of these instructive little pictures and the meaty legends on their backs. That value is clear enough in the many series which peptonize all the sciences and all the practical applications of them to the service and the extermination of man. But it may not be sufficiently realized that the common—the low-brow, if we may dare the phrase—interests of one age are the food of highbrows that come after. What value, not in money alone, would not be put upon a betting slip for one of the chariot races in the Hippodrome out of which grew those riots between the factions of the blue and the green that were among the innumerable solicitudes with which the Constantinopolitans were perturbated under Justinian? Look forward a few centuries, and aspirants for the degree of Ph.D. will be writing theses on such subjects as 'The Development of the Off-side Rule during the Reigns of Edward VII–George VI', and 'The Social and Ideological Conditions leading to the Increase of Greyhound Racing in the Third Decade of the Twentieth Century', and 'The Effect upon Municipal Administration of the Diminution of Dumps consequent upon the gradual Substitution of the Carton for the Tin'. And by that time cartophily will be not merely itself a recognized and familiar subject for examination; it will be a capital source of information about the sort of history which the civilization of the future (if there should be any left) will hold much more important and profitable than anything about Kings, Dictators, Presidents, and Generals. *The Cigarette Card* comes not a moment too soon; and the more cabinets capable of containing 52,500 cigarette cards, the greater the hope for a well-informed and wise posterity. Tobacco shares, moreover, will pay even better than they do now, unless some dastard should start selling cigarette cards without cigarettes.

HOLIDAY READING
(1932)

No question in the world—not even 'Does your mother wash?' or 'Have you given up beating your wife?'—is quite so difficult to answer straight away as 'Can you tell me of a good book to read?' That, it may be objected, is just what the professional critics are doing all day; but even the most 'impressionistic' of them—those who take the least trouble to explain why they think this book or that book what most new books seem to be, masterpieces, epoch-making, unrivalled, extraordinary, brilliant, bristling, and so forth—are addressing the public in general and not a particular person. A jest's prosperity lies in the ear of him that hears it; and the goodness of a book, in the sense intended in the question, lies in the mind of him that reads it quite as much as in the book itself. Some people want books in order to read them; but others want them to jot down their accounts in, or to make spills out of, or to use in some such ways as Samuel Butler used Frost's *Lives of Eminent Christians* in the British Museum. There are readers so voracious that they can swallow the thirty and odd fat volumes of Ruskin in a week, and for anything like a long holiday would want the entire compilations of Larousse and the Abbé Migne, and the great and beautiful *Enciclopedia Italiana*, which has published twelve huge volumes and got as far as DIR, and the complete works of Nat Gould and Edgar Wallace; and there are readers who find a single ode of Horace or page of Milton as much as they can really take in in a day; and there are readers who go to sleep so many evenings, or sunny noons, over the same page of Motley's *Dutch Republic* that the book lasts them for years. Equally, there are readers who think Sir Arthur Eddington a shallow trifler, and readers whose brains are unequal to the strain of Mr P. G. Wodehouse; and there are readers who are still shocked at George Eliot and readers who lament the Edwardian prudery of Mr Aldous Huxley. 'Can you tell me of a good book?' There can be only one answer: 'Tell me first what sort of a mind you have got to read with.'

In practice, therefore, the safest and most probably useful thing to do is that done in the 'Book List for the Holidays', which is published in this issue. These are the books, something less than one hundred in number, which, in one or other of eight categories, are attracting most attention at the moment. The regular readers of modern literature will treat the list as lovers of poetry treat anthologies; they will take note first of the items which they think ought to have been included and have not been. Of those who are not regular readers of modern literature—that is to say, of the great majority, to whom one of the charms of a holiday is the chance that it brings of more reading than is possible in work-times—some there are who, having glanced at the titles of the article, will instantly look away. It is not necessarily that they have any dislike for the 'successes of the year' or for new literature in general; but they have been longing for the holiday to come partly because they know so well what they are going to read. It is the *Aeneid*, perhaps, or some Shakespeare comedies, or *The Prelude* and *The Excursion*, or a few of the Waverleys—old friends, which can be read anew, quietly, affectionately, in the quest not first of stimulus but of soothing, of that propping of the mind of which Matthew Arnold wrote in a famous sonnet. And others there are who will scan the list eagerly in the hope of catching up with modern literature and of keeping touch with the latest manifestations of normal thought; minds keen for the excitement and refreshment of the untried. The difference between the two may depend upon a wider difference between two views about the good to be got from a holiday. To some, rest is repose; to others, it is new effort and new experience. Towards both reading can contribute very greatly, so long as it is done with good intent, and not merely, like whistling, for want of thought.

READING IN BED
(1939)

Cras leget qui nunquam legit, quique legit cras leget—or, more simply, during the present emergency those who never read in bed will take to reading in bed, and those who did read in bed will read all the more. Most people press, in poetic phrase, an earlier pillow than in peace-time, and do not fall asleep the moment they press it, to stay asleep until they are called. They will have time and desire to read. Those who are strange to the excellent habit may begin by asking their friends to recommend them a 'good' or an 'interesting' book to read, thereby dragging into the light the secret weakness of all impressionist criticism. Good, to whom? Interesting, to whom? Who shall say whether the new reader in bed will prefer John Milton or John Buchan, Dr Johnson or Dr Wodehouse? Even that great and experienced reader in bed and out of bed, Mr Holbrook Jackson, who in his *Anatomy of Bibliomania* tells of many other great readers in bed, admits that the choice of a bed book is a personal matter. His list of suitable 'works of culture or urbanity' may be of service to some hardened readers in bed, but seeing that his own favourites include the *Anthropometamorphosis* of John Bulwer, and Lovell's *Panzoologicomineralogia*, it is possible that his list might seem to the inexperienced a thought too cultured or too urbane. But he has the heart of the matter in him. He brushes aside the timorous objections—injury to eyesight, destruction of the will to sleep, and danger of fire through mishap to candle or lamp (small indeed, in these days of electric light, but has he forgotten what happened to Dr Folliott's cook in Peacock's *Crotchet Castle*?); and he knows that, to enjoy reading in bed to the full, the reader must be conscious of his bed as well as of his book. Those who habitually fall asleep in libraries, which is the converse of reading in bed, say the same about the armchair.

Reading in Bed

The truth is that what to read in bed is not nearly so important as how to read in bed. Once the technique has been mastered, the question whether to read in bed is not difficult to settle. It only arises when the sleeper wakes about half-way between bed-time and getting-up time, and must make up his mind whether he is sleepy enough to drop off again soon or wide enough awake to be a hero and extract some portion of his upper self from the snugness of the bed-clothes. But it is none too easy for each reader to find the precise method of reading in bed which is best for himself. Mr Holbrook Jackson's favourite bed books sound like tall folios or fat quartos in leather bindings; and other readers in bed find anything heavier than a World's Classic or an Everyman a crushing weight. Big books, moreover, take two hands, and one of the nicer points of the art of reading in bed is to keep one hand warm under the clothes, while the other does all the work, holding the book and turning the pages—preferably with the thumb from the bottom, but, in case of emergency, with help from the nose, or even the tongue. Position counts for more than half the battle. Some find themselves happily conscious of the bed as well as of the book only if they lie flat on their backs and take special measures (a woolly or a bed-jacket) to keep their arms and hands warm—and it is always through the arms that the reader in bed catches cold. Others develop complicated schemes for curling up on their sides; and a reader has been known to claim that he could keep himself entirely covered, except for his head above the eyes, and still keep his book always in the light and turn its pages without exposing a hand.

A very nice point in the art is knowing when to stop. To stop too soon may be to lie awake but in no mood to face the bother of starting all over again. To go on too long may be to dispel the gathering drowsiness—which is all very well for the student but a mere blunder in the reader for pleasure; or it may be to fall asleep, spectacles on nose and light burning, which must lead in an hour or two to an uncomfortable and ashamed awakening. Those, therefore, who are taking to reading in bed for the first time have some interesting problems to solve before they are adept at the art; and their adventures may double the old hand's thankfulness that his diligence in the past has made him master of one of life's purest pleasures.

THE DECAY OF THE MUSIC-HALL
(1942)

Many a young brow, high or low, will have been wrinkled in perplexity at recent complaints by Sir Max Beerbohm to the world in general, and by Mr Charles B. Cochran and others to readers of *The Times*, about the dearth, decay, decline, or other default in the art of the music-hall. When we are thirsting for music, asks the highbrow, what do we get on the wireless but music-hall, music-hall, music-hall? When we are really enjoying ourselves, grumbles the lowbrow, they stop a perfectly good music-hall programme and turn on that ghastly classical stuff. To the veteran it will be clear that on neither side do the young people know what they are talking about. If Home and Forces were both filled from end to end with music-hall turns (as now and then they threaten to be) no mere listener could get any idea of the art of the music-hall. To hear a music-hall song without seeing the singer is not even to hear it, much less to take it in. The veteran will remember how he has heard one song by one singer at two music-halls—one more 'West End' than the other. The words were the same; the tune was the same; the song was not one but two. The West End version would have seemed very dull at the other house; what the homelier audience enjoyed would have shocked a part of the other, and the whole might have combined—as audiences will—to hiss and boo. So little in proportion depended on the words and the tune, so much on the personality and the art of the performer. First and

most powerful was his mere physical presence; and next this
pause, that gesture, the other glance. There, not in words or
tune, lay the song—the work of art. And none who remem-
bers that great genius Miss Marie Lloyd could have any doubt
what significance could lie in even an abstention from a smile
or a wink.

So that, when Mr Cochran writes that the music-hall was
killed by the 'refeened' drawing-room turn, with lampshades
and aspidistras, he speaks truth. But how was it that lampshades and aspidistras penetrated the music-hall, as German
and Japanese 'experts' penetrate a doomed country? It was
part of a wider development that included the emancipation of
women and the social whitewashing of the entertaining pro-
fessions. The theatre's turn had come earlier. Mr and Mrs
Bancroft had carried West End manners into a stronghold of
the popular art, the 'Dust Hole', in a by-street off the Tot-
tenham Court Road. After that it was easy for Hare, Kendal,
and the others to smarten up the profession (and no one has
suggested more persuasively than Sir Max Beerbohm that on
the whole that may not have been very good for the art of
acting). From another angle Stewart Headlam and his Church
and Stage Guild reached inviting hands to the variety people.
Chorus girls and dancing girls were asked to tea, and the
clergy house of the now demolished church of St Mary in
Charing Cross Road was a headquarters in the centre of the
district. Meanwhile in the naughty, *fin-de-siècle*, and otherwise disturbing nineties well-bred women grew sick of staying
at home when their brothers and so on went out to 'vulgar'
places of amusement. They demanded to be taken too. The
hour was propitious, and 'nice' women began to come to the
music-hall, where the clergy were already at home.

No doubt it was wise of the music-hall to do what the
theatre had done and take advantage of the new public. The
scope of the effects could hardly have been foreseen. Tobacco
alone made the atmosphere of, say, the Oxford or the Tivoli
a little strong for the late-Victorian lady, and structural im-
provements led in time to Morton's Palace and other palatial

variety houses of which music-hall was a misnomer. What mattered much more was the change in the programme. It was a long way from the one artist before any old backcloth to the alabaster-stalled Handel Festival sort of female choir among the palms and the aspidistras on either side of the stage of the new Coliseum and between them not a song and a singer but a 'song-scena' and a crowd. Having a new public, the variety stage was only too eager (the old mistake of theatrical management) to give it what it was supposed to want. But the art of the music-hall was thus driven out and driven down. With this change morals and even taste had very little to do. Not many years later, after the war, scarce a lady in the land would have turned a hair at the ripest of the jokes or hints of the comedian in full career; and indeed there was not much for the normally squeamish to complain of. What hampered the artists of either sex was no distrust of their own standards of decency, which they knew and observed. It was the warning brought by the lampshade-and-aspidistra turns— that their public was not now their old public, looking to them for the old fun and agreed upon the same conventions. The music-hall was feeling its share of a wide social change; and with his freedom the music-hall artist lost the command of his personality, which was the core of his art.

WHAT IS FRANCE?

(March 1940)

The same word spoken, or merely thought over and over again will induce, as hypnotists know, a queer state of mind in which it seems to have no meaning. During the last six months one word has been repeating itself over and over again (though perhaps not so regularly as it should have done) in the ears and minds of us all; and then some occasion—such as the appearance this week of our Special Correspondent's two articles on 'The

French at War'—suddenly makes ear or mind aware of that persistent repetition. 'France—France—France'—the sound (and a musical sound it is) has been ringing so constantly that it has begun to be taken for granted. 'France—France—France'—but what is it that the sound means? When we read 'France', or say 'France', or hear 'France', what is there beyond the musical sound? What, so to speak, *is* France, apart from the sound?

The search for the answer is one of the most breathlessly exciting and desperately disappointing adventures possible. Certainly there will be a terrific run after the quarry, and just as certainly, when hounds are at its throat, the white doe will disappear into the impenetrable forest and be no more seen. For the average Englishman the safest start is by the map. In the year blank he knew the boy's (half-regretful) thrill of seeing where the Bastille used to stand and spotting the famous gargoyle on Notre Dame; and not long afterwards his Paris expanded to include Fontainebleau and Versailles and Saint-Germain. Then, perhaps, came golf and bathing on the north coast; the castles of the Loire; the cathedrals; the time when he fancied that he knew Provence because, besides Avignon and Arles and Nîmes, he had been to Les Saintes Maries and Aigues-Mortes and seen Les Baux by moonlight; and those silvan days on the east when he only wanted to look at the far snowy Alps because that was the best way of enjoying the lakes and forests and the climbing roads of France. And alongside the places that he has seen—many of them perhaps found by accident, unknown by name, full of beauty, of kindly people and of comfort—there come crowding the places that he has not seen but has vowed to see—this castle, that cathedral, that hotel (where he that knows how to ask for it will get a bottle of that burgundy), that hill-town where, with no help from any product of the *vendange*, the children and the climbing roses have, as men say, a finer than terrestrial beauty. *Il faut en finir*—and then he will be able to go there.

This geographical investigation of the word 'France' makes easy going for the start, but there is far more difficult country ahead. Most Englishmen 'learnt French' at school; and the meaning of 'France' may involve every step taken since, well grounded in *Le Roi des Montagnes* (or was it perhaps *Les Silences du Colonel Bramble?*), he adventured alone into Gaboriau, or *Les Trois Mousquetaires*, or perhaps *Arsène Lupin*, and so began goodness knows what pilgrimage in which he came upon Molière and Montaigne (somehow always contriving to by-pass Corneille and Racine), was bludgeoned by Balzac, beached on the sandy shallows of Proust, and—in the Englishman's regular course—tickled to death by Anatole France and reverentially bored to death by certain others. France, too, connotes a great deal about painting; and the passage from boyish loves like Bouguereau or Meissonier through Impressionists and Post-impressionists and goodness knows what else cannot but be full of detail; just as the theatrical passage from Sarah Bernhardt as Phèdre and Coquelin as Tartuffe to Sacha Guitry and the moderns must be full of detail. The danger is—especially if we take in food and contrast a *blini au caviare* with the homely Shrove Tuesday pancake at the vicarage—that the crowding detail will prevent the emergence of any single vision that can give a meaning to this empty word, and stand, however vaguely, for France. Even the personal element may fail us. How to reconcile a sentimentality over white hairs and childhood (especially female) that a Victorian Adelphi gallery would have considered sloppy, with a bureaucratic rigidity that makes even the bargain basements of Whitehall seem enlightened and accommodating? How can prodigality of personal attention and service live in the same bosom as Harpagon, all claws for the uttermost farthing?

But to ask such questions is to ask why, in these matters, as in the arts, in eating and drinking, in everything, France is not England. Let the cloud of detail settle, and above it some image begins to stand out. What we feared has happened. The white doe has escaped, bearing with her certain qualities we well wot of, adamantine hardness, crystal clearness, unalterable resolution, that this clumsy, individual hunting could never hope to catch. But something of the vision may be remembered. Thus hastily judged by experience, France stands for England's practical example of a society in the main like herself but more finely and consciously civilized. The Victorian cartoonists went wrong in particulars, not in direction, when they opposed the natty little short-skirted lady to lumpish slow-moving John Bull. At any rate the individual Englishman will have gone some way towards finding a good answer to the question 'What is France?' if, next time it occurs, he can answer thus —France is the composite of human beings, arts, and scenes which has shed all this light upon my life and has helped me so graciously to see where I wanted to go.

COURAGE TO BELIEVE

(*July 1940*)

Recent events have put a wholesome check on the 'wishful thinking' of the easy-going and the ill-informed; and the evil spirit whose breath is negation is looking eagerly to see the next effect—the overthrow of the faith of those whose faith was well founded and firmly built. That evil spirit will be disappointed. This man and that man may prove to be broken reeds and pierce the hand that leaned on them. This class or that class, even this people or that people, may suffer the inner self-mistrust which betrays them to outer compulsion, and still the faith holds firm. It is not a faith in men, in classes, or in nations at any and every moment. It is a faith in the essential quality of human nature and in its power to rise again out of no matter what spiritual degradation and material disaster. Those who had the courage to have faith before the blows fell have it still unshaken, and all the tougher for the momentary strain. Defying the fiend, they are beyond his power. Nevertheless, that evil spirit is not going all unsatisfied. If he cannot gloat over true faith turned into despair, he is watching with glee the fate of men of little faith, men of pretended faith, and men of no faith. These, who 'shrink up from existence', as Blake put it, are always resentful of anything that disturbs their quiet existence within the shell of negation that wards off feeling and impulse. Distrusting themselves and fearing the forces of life, they welcome the present abundant occasion for sneering that faith and aspiration, devotion and sacrifice are all humbug; that no expression of faith, in word or in deed, can be sincere; and that any such manifestation is a trick, devised by those in power to delude innocent minds for selfish ends.

Never before, no doubt, has there been so much excuse for this mistrust. Systematic and elaborated lying has debased the whole currency of truth. And, besides the public pronouncements which have shaken the public confidence in official truth, there is all the buzzing of the poisonous flies of private rumour and surreptitious suggestion of the false. The correction of this prevalent wrong will certainly not be one of the lightest of tasks in the future reconstruction of the world—or, rather, in the construction of a new and decent world. By the most scrupulous abstention from any twisting of the truth to party or personal ends, any suppression of the necessary truth and any ambiguous statement of the truth, Governments and Press, statesmen, officials, and private persons must all labour to clear away the reproach. The evil spirit, no doubt, will not easily be driven out of the minds of men; and it will take some perseverance to restore the general will to believe in truth and the honesty of vision that will recognize truth when it is encountered. But there will be little hope for recovery even in a world normally at peace unless the lie can be known for a lie and fall dead and ineffectual from the lips of the liar.